"Isn't He Gorgeous?" Louie Mouthed as I Stood Gawking.

He brushed by me without a glance, but the brown bag with Louie's bologna sandwich slipped from my hands. Potato chips, orange, sandwich, and cookies scattered on the wooden floor. The Pepsi can rolled under the nail rack. Then he was on his knees helping me.

"Beth!" screamed Louie. "That was my lunch!"

"Hi, I'm Jason Teasdale," he said, scooping up the crushed chips. His voice had a rich, sure timbre that I recognized as Tourist, First Class. His eyes were ice blue, clear and hard as glass, but sexy!

The bologna stuck to the side of a shelf like wet rubber. He laughed while I peeled it off. I noticed his eyes deepen when he smiled. Our heads were so close they seemed to be touching. I felt a funny quiver in my stomach.

"Who are *you*?"

"She's my baby sister, Beth," said Louie. She emphasized the word "baby." "And you, squirt," she said, "owe me lunch."

"You don't look like a squirt to me," said Jason. And if I didn't know it before, I knew it then. I was smitten.

BYE BYE Miss AMERICAN PIE

JAN GREENBERG

AN ARCHWAY PAPERBACK
Published by POCKET BOOKS • NEW YORK

Lines from "American Pie" by Don McLean
© 1971 by Mayday Music (a division of
Merit Music Corporation) and Benny Bird
Music (BMI). Used by permission.

An Archway Paperback published by
POCKET BOOKS, a division of Simon & Schuster, Inc.
1230 Avenue of the Americas, New York, N.Y. 10020

Copyright © 1985 by Jan Greenberg
Cover artwork copyright © 1986 Frank Morris

Published by arrangement with Farrar, Straus & Giroux, Inc.
Library of Congress Catalog Card Number: 85-47590

ISBN: 0-671-62186-6

First Archway Paperback printing June, 1986

10 9 8 7 6 5 4 3 2

AN ARCHWAY PAPERBACK and colophon are
registered trademarks of Simon & Schuster, Inc.

Printed in the U.S.A.

For Larry and Sandra,
Bob and Maureen,
Harold and Elaine
and Faye
with love and appreciation

BYE BYE Miss AMERICAN PIE

1

MY MOTHER named me Beth after her favorite character in *Little Women*. It's spooky to be compared to somebody out of a novel, especially one who ends up dying, sweet and innocent to the very end.

"The name suits you perfectly," my parents tell me. What they mean is that I'm supposed to be sweet and innocent, too. To the very end. So far, I haven't disappointed them. But beneath the surface, I like to tell myself, lurks a wild and woolly beast. Whenever my mother says, "Meet my daughter, she's just like Beth in *Little Women*," I have the urge to leap, beat my chest, and snort like an orangutan. Instead, I smile politely and endure the inevitable pat on the head.

"Gross," said my older sister, Louie, the last time Mother fussed over me in public. "Why don't you tell her to cut it out?"

"Beth's not a two-year-old, Motherrr," Louie added. "Stop babying her." Louie was named after the author of *Little Women*, Louisa May Alcott, and true to her namesake, she has an editorial comment about everything. Only my parents call her by her given name. Everyone else calls her Louie.

"Beth will always be my baby," retorted Mother. Some baby! I'm fifteen years old. But my long hair and freckles make me look as if I'm still twelve. Louie's eighteen and looks thirty. I'm also short, which is definitely not an advantage in a tall world. I get claustrophobia in crowds and strain my neck looking up. My legs dangle over chairs, and I can't reach the top shelf in my closet, even when I stand on tiptoe. Whatever junk I've piled up there lands on my head. Fairy tales with elves and dwarfs give me nightmares. I'm four foot eleven and I'd gladly trade places with a giant, just to avoid being treated like one of the ceramic knick-knacks on my mother's mantel.

The problem is that people are always trying to take care of me, especially my mother. But she has another reason for being overprotective. If I turn out all right, it will make up for the fact that my sister drives her crazy. They fight constantly. This morning, for example, Louie swaggered into the kitchen wearing a purple sweater and a yellow mini-skirt. Her red hair was fluffed out on one side and slicked back on the other.

"You're not going to work dressed like that, are you?" Mother asked, wringing out the dishcloth with unusual vigor.

Here we go again, I thought. It was too early for an argument, so I tried to distract them. I scooted my chair in front of Louie to block Mother's view. The legs squeaked across the linoleum. "Here comes the hobby horse," I said, plunking myself and the chair in the middle of the room.

"You are so infantile," Louie groaned, but she was half smiling.

"Any more bacon, Mom? It was delicious."

Mother smiled at me, too. "No, honey. It's all gone."

"Thanks for saving me a piece, squirt," grumped Louie. She sashayed around my chair and planted herself at the door in a chorus-girl pose. "What's wrong with this outfit, anyway?" I started to laugh until I saw my father's face frowning behind her.

"A proper young lady doesn't go around town dressed like a hooker," he said, pushing past her and sinking heavily into his chair. "I won't have you working at our store in that getup."

"You two are still in the Middle Ages," Louie shouted. "I'm not changing. No way! Besides," she added, before she grabbed my toast and stomped out, "you need me there today. You're shorthanded." It's easy to be the good one with Louie around.

Even when we were little, Louie had a knack for getting in trouble. While I joined the Campfire Girls, sang in the choir, cross-stitched, and played jacks, she tore around town on her bicycle, hung out at the video-game center, and spied on tourists in hotel lobbies. As far as she was concerned, I was a nuisance, the brat who tagged along behind her until she was forced to yell, "Get lost, squirt." Then I'd escape to my hideaway, the storage closet, where I spent endless hours drawing squiggly designs with my Magic Markers. Ear pressed to the wall, I'd listen to Louie telling secrets to her friends.

In those days, she had the look of an alley cat—a scraggly kid with a mean squint and matted hair. But no longer. Now she's a beauty, more like a Persian cat. But sometimes I think her instincts are still those of a stray. In my case, as the poet Emily Dickinson wrote, "My life has been too simple and stern to embarrass any." I've graduated from jacks to crossword puzzles, from Magic Markers to pastels. But I've never gotten over the feeling that most people prefer my sister to me because she's more exciting.

On Saturdays, Louie works at the hardware store with Mom and Dad. I stay at home doing chores. It's my way of avoiding the store. Practically every time I walk in the place, my eyes start to water or I have a sneezing fit. When I watch my parents and Louie bustling about filling orders and shouting questions at each other, I feel like a stranger in a strange land.

This morning, as usual, my parents rushed off to work and I had the house to myself. The rooms were filled with familiar sounds—the clock ticking on the mantel, the steam iron hissing, baby squirrels squealing in the rafters. Why is it always a relief to be here alone? Maybe in some ways, I *am* like Beth in *Little Women*, "the cricket on the hearth, content to stay at home."

It took nearly two hours to clean house and do the ironing. I moved from room to room in a mindless rhythm. Afterward I found a spot to sit and started sketching whatever caught my eye—the coffee table with its wooden bowl of cashews and glass ashtray, an open book, and even the blue-and-white squares of the polished linoleum floor. I don't remember a time when I didn't have a crayon or pencil in my hand.

Every Saturday, I stop by the store to bring Louie her lunch. Reluctantly, I put my charcoals and sketch pad in the storage closet.

Twelve-thirty. A windy day. We live in a resort town on the southern tip of Florida. Two types can be found in Sand Key—the rich tourists who stay in fancy hotels or buy condos on the beach and the townies. Our family has lived here for three generations. That's a status symbol in Palm

4

Beach or Miami. But in Sand Key, it spells TOWNY, the lowest of the low.

The cost of living is high because of the tourist trade. According to my father, our hardware store does just enough business to make ends meet. My parents yell at Louie, who spends every dime she earns on trendy clothes, records, and cosmetics, and I really can't blame them.

Just as I turned the corner, I heard the roar of a loud motor, and a boy on a shiny new Harley Davidson motorcycle came speeding toward me. He weaved in and out of cars as if they were obstacles on a course.

Mrs. Walker rushed out of the laundry and waved her fist. People honked their horns and yelled from windows. A tourist in a black lace beach coat tilted her oversized sunglasses to get a better look. Down Main Street blared the warning signal of Officer Muncie's patrol car. The boy turned once to wave in Muncie's direction, taunting him to catch up. As the siren grew louder, the motorcycle moved faster. It practically flew, leaving a trail of exhaust fumes and dust. I stood mesmerized until the last cloud of smoke dissolved.

The motorcyclist was either a daredevil or a complete maniac. When he passed, I noticed the way he leaned forward, his hands clenching the handlebars as if he was riding to fall. Louie would call him "gorgeous." The combination of gorgeous and dangerous is sexy enough on TV or in movies, but in real life, it's irresistible. I wondered who he was.

After about a block, I usually begin my delaying tactics. First I sit on the curb and meditate; then I wander into the drugstore and flip through magazines. I'm always hopeful that I'll run into someone I know for a prolonged conversation. Today, I decided to daydream about the boy on the motorcycle. But just as I found a spot under a palm tree, my friend Andy Kohn showed up. "I spotted you from my window," he said. "You're walking at your usual snail's pace."

"Of course! I'm on my way to the store." I waved my bag.

"Little Red Riding Hood bringing Granny her goodies?"

I nodded. "Louie, alias the Big Bad Wolf." Andy's my best friend, so he knows how I feel about her. When he sank down next to me and stretched his legs out, his jeans wrinkled up to his knees. He wears his slacks too short, to give the impression he's growing taller. But in reality, he's almost my height. Louie calls us the Wimps of Sandstone High.

"This school has two sane, straight people," Andy once said. "You and me."

"Don't forget brilliant and honest," I added.

Andy and I met in the lunch line last year. We were last in line because we're the only ones who won't push and shove to get there first. It took us a long time to reach the food, but we'd already started a conversation that isn't finished yet.

"You wouldn't believe what Hurricane Lucy did now," he said, referring to his mother, who was thirty when Andy was born. Now she's forty-five, and according to him, it's been downhill all the way. Secretly I think she was brilliant to have a baby after she finished law school. However, Andy sees himself as the beleaguered only child. "She offered my services to the family next door."

"You mean the one with six poodles?"

"Exactly."

"What services?"

"You're looking at an official dog walker. For twenty-five cents a mutt, I have to walk them twice a day. They're disgusting. For little dogs, they leave dinosaur droppings. I have to follow behind them with a damn pooper-scooper and clean the mess." He held his nose.

I cracked up. Andy smiled for a moment, then he went back to ranting and raving. "You'd think they'd fence in their yard. But no! So good old Mrs. Kohn volunteers her son, the neighborhood Boy Scout." He shrugged, a look of resignation on his face.

"You won't get rich. That's for sure."

"This could turn me into a hardened criminal," he sighed.

"Enough chitchat," I said, springing up. "Off to the salt mines."

"They haven't put you to work there, have they?" asked Andy.

"Not yet, but I can feel it coming," I said. Louie seemed to be getting on their nerves more and more these days.

"I'll come by later with my new friends," Andy called after me.

Grains of sand blew in my eyes. The air was so heavy I practically had to push my way to the side street off Main, where Goodall Hardware has stood for twenty years. The store is white stucco, a two-story building like most of the architecture in Sand Key. Even the hotels look as if they came off the same drawing board. If my parents painted the front turquoise, it might make for a little variety. As it is now, the only distinguishing features are a wrought-iron balcony overgrown with ivy, and sacks of premix cement piled high on the wooden porch.

When I went inside, Louie was checking items at the cash register. The way she checked each item twice before ringing it up, you'd think people were purchasing diamonds and gold instead of nails and thumbtacks. My parents were deep in conversation with some customers, who demand more than their fair share of free advice. Their questions range from how to repair their roofs to the intricacies of unstopping a toilet. My father's an expert on home repair, plumbing, electricity, camping, gardening, and so on. My mother's a walking encyclopedia of household hints. The Heloise of Sand Key. She can save money on gas bills, demonstrate how to eliminate nasty stains and household odors, and prevent mildew. My mechanical skills are limited to changing a light bulb and hammering in a nail. I can't tell a cotter pin from a wing nut, a stove bolt from a lock washer. The whole store with its jumbled rows of brushes, scissors, assorted nuts, screws, and pipes, ladders, hoses, and tools promises a future of domestic efficiency and safety. Unfortunately, it's a future my parents have determined for me, one that is as automatic and predictable as the equipment they sell. But my sister's in her element here.

Louie was so absorbed in her work that she failed to notice me or a boy who stood outside the window looking in at her. When I recognized him, I felt strangely excited. There he was, the one on the motorcycle. He pushed through the screen door and headed straight for my sister. Curious, I backed myself into a corner between the counter and the shelves to watch. Louie continued itemizing Mrs. Casey's toilet articles and pretended not to notice. He drummed his fingers on the counter until she finally turned to face him, one hand on her hip in her typical provocative pose. She twirled a lock of red hair around her finger and puckered her lips like Marilyn Monroe.

"Yeo, babe," he said.

"I'm busy," she told him. He leaned over and whispered in her ear. Louie shrugged. A customer, loaded down with cans of paint, dumped them on the counter. "I've gotta work," Louie said. "Maybe I'll see you later." Maybe? I thought. Is she losing her marbles? He smiled a lazy smile and waved goodbye. Louie flipped her ponytail and looked away. For a moment I hated my sister for being brassy, so sure of herself.

"Isn't he gorgeous?" she mouthed as I stood gawking.

He brushed by me without a glance, but the brown bag with Louie's bologna sandwich slipped from my hands. Potato chips, orange, sandwich, and cookies scattered on the wooden floor. The Pepsi can rolled under the nail rack. Then he was on his knees helping me.

"Beth!" screamed Louie. "That was my lunch!"

"Hi, I'm Jason Teasdale," he said, scooping up the crushed chips. His voice had a rich, sure timbre that I recognized as Tourist, First Class. His eyes were ice-blue, clear and hard as glass, but sexy!

The bologna stuck to the side of a shelf like wet rubber. He laughed while I peeled it off. I noticed his eyes deepen when he smiled. Our heads were so close they seemed to be touching. I felt a funny quiver in my stomach.

"Who are *you*?"

Quickly I stood, clutching the ripped bag, feeling like a little brown wren with a little brown bag.

"She's my *baby* sister, Beth," said Louie, who was checking items and watching us at the same time. Pointing at me, she said, "And you, squirt, owe me lunch."

"You don't look like a squirt to me," said Jason. And if I didn't know it before, I knew it then—I was smitten.

Louie interrupted. "I'm starving. Go to the market and get me some food. While you're at it, here's Mother's shopping list. I won't have time later." She always suckers me into doing her household jobs, but this time she seemed a little too eager to get rid of me.

Louie motioned me out as if she were shooing a fly. I left

feeling just as insignificant, without even nodding goodbye to Jason. If I looked him in the eye, I might blush or stammer like one of those dumb girls in Harlequin novels.

The sun was bright and hot on Main Street. The wind whistled, so gusty that palm trees lining the streets seemed to bend and shake like exotic dancers. October weather is unpredictable. One day it's overcast and cool; the next, windy and humid. No one goes to the beach on windy days except me. I spend hours there searching for bits of colored glass rubbed smooth by the sea and sand. My collection of glass fills a large wicker basket in my room. Sometimes I climb a high boulder and sketch. The beach offers endless possibilities—especially on this kind of a day. But Louie's list would keep me busy most of the afternoon.

Out of the corner of my eye, I spotted Jason leaving the store. Then, as I crossed the street, I felt him at my elbow, but I kept right on walking, eyes straight ahead. I was filled with a kind of odd sensation that made my knees weak, as if I were on the verge of some new, strange land, one with rocky cliffs, huge jungle ferns, and dark stretches of sand.

"Louie's baby sister needs an escort. May I accompany you to the supermarché?" asked Jason in a formal tone. Only a rich kid would give Mr. Olsen's market a fancy French name. Maybe I was being too sensitive, but the tourists have always looked down on the townies. I decided to ignore him.

"Hey," he asked, following me through the revolving door, "are you shy, or don't you like me?"

"I like you." I attempted to smile the way girls do in lipstick commercials. My lips felt sticky, pasted on my face.

"That's more like it." He gave me a friendly nudge.

"I've seen you before," I said. "About an hour ago riding your motorcycle. You caused an uproar."

"Did I?" he asked, surprised. "I was busy trying to get away from your trusty law enforcer. That guy doesn't give me a break." He unzipped his jacket. I wondered why he was wearing a coat when it was 75 degrees. The wind wasn't that strong.

I rolled a cart up and down the aisle and pretended to concentrate on the price of vegetables. Jason stayed by my side, chatting away as if I were an old friend.

"My folks have a place on the beach. They come during Christmas vacation. Right now they're on a safari in Africa. My father sees himself as the great white hunter." He laughed harshly. I pictured his father, maybe an older version of Jason, wearing white shorts and a pith helmet. "I got in some trouble at boarding school. Couldn't get hold of them, so I came down early."

I wondered what kind of trouble he meant, but decided not to ask. If he wanted to tell me, he would. Besides, having a nosy mother had taught me to respect other people's privacy. Yet everything about Jason aroused my curiosity.

"So now that I'm here, what do you do for fun in this town?"

I had to laugh. "I spend my free time at the beach sketching or collecting glass. But I guess that's not what you meant."

"Well . . . not exactly." All the while we were talking, he strolled next to me, picking up items, turning them over in his hands, and putting them down elsewhere. "But," he continued, "I happen to know a little about art. My folks collect French paintings and used to drag me to every museum and gallery in Europe."

"You're lucky," I said. "I've never been outside the state of Florida."

"I never looked at it that way," he said, "especially the

11

time I got lost in the Louvre. I ended up crying in front of the *Mona Lisa* until a guard rescued me.''

"Poor thing," I teased. "I really feel sorry for you."

"Listen, I'd love to see your pictures. I'll bet you're really good," Jason said.

"Not too many kids around here are interested in art," I admitted, feeling shy and excited at the same time. "Maybe one of these days I'll show them to you."

By that time, we were at the checkout station. As I stacked my purchases on the counter, Jason wandered away. But outside the market, he turned up at my side again. "How about steak for dinner?" he said.

"I only wish," I said. "Steak's too expensive." He gave me a funny look. "I guess 'too expensive's' not in your vocabulary." The tourist mentality bothers me.

"There are tricks to beat inflation, that's all," he said. Unzipping his jacket, he revealed a package of strip steaks, a can of artichoke hearts, and two Snickers bars.

"You have to be crazy," I hissed, a queasy feeling building up in my stomach.

"Are you going to tell?" His eyes were strangely bright and there was a tight smile on his face.

"Of course not. What do you take me for? I'd never tell. Why should I?" I sniffed. "You're just a big show-off."

He smiled. "Maybe I think you're worth showing off for." Then he winked and sauntered away, leaving me staring until he was out of sight.

2

THAT NIGHT Mother made shepherd's pie for dinner. As I glopped the lumpy potatoes on my plate, I wondered if Jason was enjoying his stolen steak. I squeezed into the booth Dad built in the corner of our small kitchen and gave him a hug. When I was little, he used to grab me and waltz around the room. Once, during one of these whirls, I nicked my cheek on his belt buckle, but I didn't want to spoil his fun by crying. Today he was so preoccupied he forgot to hug me back.

"Louisa," Mother yelled up the stairs, "dinner's ready." No response.

"She's probably on the phone again," said Dad. He picked up the receiver and growled, "Get down here. Now!" and slammed it down.

Ten seconds later, Louie burst in, wrapped in a terry-cloth robe. "You don't have to embarrass me in front of my friends."

"Nice of you to dress for dinner," Dad said dryly. She gave him a dirty look.

Every single night at supper there's a feeling of tension. It hangs over us like a gray cloud.

"He was just kidding," I interjected. But whatever Dad says makes Louie mad, and vice versa. She picked at her food.

"Louisa, you're not touching your dinner. I swear you're going to become skinny as a rail," Mother said.

I ate quickly and went back for seconds. I didn't want Mother to feel badly that no one was eating. But her casseroles taste as if she scrambles all the leftovers in a blender and forgets to take them out of the oven on time.

"How can you eat that stuff?" complained Louie.

"Don't insult your mother," Dad said.

"Today was such a slow day at the store," said Mother, changing the subject. "People were doing more looking than buying."

Dad nodded. "If business continues to slump, I'll be forced to have a sale before Christmas."

"When I went over the inventory today," said Mother, "I noticed we were missing a bunch of items from the tool department."

"I think I lose five percent a year from theft alone," complained Dad, as I squirmed in my seat. I quickly cleared the table and rinsed the dishes. Louie sat diddling with her spoon, an odd expression on her face.

"You ought to stop selling expensive items that can be ripped off," she blurted. "Besides, it takes too long to talk people into buying them."

"I enjoy talking to customers," Dad said. "I've known most of them all my life."

"Well, there's no profit in it," Louie said crossly. "It's not worth the trouble."

"Louisa, I don't need your advice on how to run my business."

Louie threw down her napkin. "You make less than five dollars on a chain saw that takes over thirty minutes to sell. I don't get your attitude."

"I run a family business," Dad said indignantly. Mother nodded.

Louie cut in, "But the money's in commercial clients."

"Well, go work in one of those damn shopping centers that sell orders for nails over the telephone all day and see how you like it," said Dad, which made Louie's face red with anger. She shoved her chair back and stomped out. I followed her to our room.

"I'm sick of him putting me down," Louie said. "I work hard at that stupid store."

"He knows that," I offered weakly. But the truth was that Dad hardly noticed all the extra jobs Louie did.

"Well, I'm fed up. I'm getting out of here tonight."

"Where are you going?"

"Remember that gorgeous boy I was talking to this afternoon? He invited me over for dinner. He lives in a fantastic house."

"So that's why you didn't eat. I bet I know what's on the menu tonight." Louie looked puzzled, but I didn't elaborate.

"You're not supposed to go out with guys they don't know," I told her.

"Well, keep quiet about it," she ordered. "They don't care, anyway. I'll tell Dad that Susie Sloan is having kids over." She checked her makeup in the mirror. Somehow the thought of Louie and Jason together bothered me.

As if she could read my mind, Louie whirled around. "Hey, Beth, do me a favor? Come with me. If you're along, they won't give me a hard time."

"I can't," I said, turning the idea over in my head, an

15

image of the three of us, Jason and Louie on one side of the room, me on the other.

"Why not? We'll have fun. You should get out more, anyway."

"I'll feel dumb, out of place."

"If Mom calls Susie's and I'm not there, I'll be grounded." Louie grabbed my hands and pulled me off the bed. "Come on. You'll love it."

"You must be losing your mind," I said. But I stuffed my sketch pad in my purse and followed her downstairs.

"Let's not show up at Jason's on the bus like two nerds," whispered Louie. "Ask Dad if we can have the car. He won't give it to me."

"All right. All right. Just promise to drive carefully. Last time you used the car, you smashed into a stop sign. They can't keep fixing your dents."

Hunched over his desk in the living room, Dad was so busy paying the bills he didn't argue too much when I asked for the car. "Beth, see that Louisa sticks to the speed limit," he said, tossing me the keys. "Be back by eleven-thirty."

"Fat chance," murmured Louie, who hadn't been home before one in months.

The brakes screeched as she backed out of the driveway.

"Take it easy, will you!" We bickered and laughed all the way across town.

"I wish I were as relaxed as you around boys," I told her. I've only had one official date and that was with Andy Kohn. Strictly platonic, so it didn't count.

"You must be joking," my sister said. She threw her head back and laughed. Louie's laugh is husky and deep. I've tried to imitate it, but mine comes out sounding hoarse, as if I have an awful cold.

16

"Louie, you laugh the way you act—totally uninhibited. I sound as if I've just swallowed a frog."

"Beth, I love the way you giggle. It's never fake."

"Really?"

Louie reached over and poked me in the ribs.

"Stop it," I squealed, "I'm ticklish."

"See, you have a cute laugh," Louie said.

"Cute, but definitely not sexy."

"Well," said my sister in an exaggerated husky voice, "you be cute. Leave sexy to me . . . especially tonight."

Oh boy, I thought, how am I going to get through this?

As we turned on the outer beach road, the houses grew bigger, the lawns wider.

"Here it is. Number 4," announced Louie, swerving onto a driveway edged with tall palm trees. We parked our beat-up Chevy next to a shiny new Jaguar, then stood for a moment and took in the house. "It's really something, isn't it?" breathed Louie, who's usually not in awe of anything.

The house was all glass and poured concrete. Lights blazed inside, and we could see a winding staircase leading up three levels. Earthenware pots filled with red geraniums lined the stairs. The house shimmered with streaks of light like a diamond with a hundred facets. The starry sky held a sliver of moon. I could hear the sound of waves breaking on the beach. I inhaled the damp, salty air.

"Here are the keys," said Louie. "Why don't you take the car and go to the library or something? Pick me up at one."

"Hey, wait a minute. My coming along on this nocturnal visit was your idea. Besides, I don't have a license."

"I've changed my mind," said Louie. "Go play with your little friend Andy."

"Don't get sarcastic about my friends, Louie," I yelled. "Yours aren't so great."

17

"Well, if you don't like my friends, then you won't mind leaving. Now!"

Suddenly the glass door swung open. Jason stood there holding a beer.

"What are you two making so much noise about? Stop screaming at each other and come in. I'm about to burn the steak." Louie gave me a warning look, as if to say "I'll get you for this," and swept grandly into the house. She began marching around as if she owned the place. Ignoring me, she tucked her hand through Jason's arm.

"How about a drink and a guided tour? In that order."

"Sure. Come on, Beth," he called to me. Louie made herself at home by stretching out on the couch, while I hung back at the door. "Hope you girls are hungry."

"I'm not," I said stiffly. "Where's the television? There's a program I don't want to miss."

Louie's face softened. "Give Beth a soda and let's eat," she said.

"At your service," Jason said, pressing a button which opened a panel, revealing a fully stocked bar. The Stones blared in the background. The house reminded me of a movie set.

Behind Jason, Louie motioned me out. I imagined myself making a grand exit. Instead, I muttered, "Well, *Three's Company* is just about to begin, so . . ."

"It sure is," snickered Louie, converting the laugh I'd admired into a derisive cackle.

"The TV's down the hall to the left," said Jason, as if he couldn't care less whether I was there or not.

I found a small study lined with bookcases holding matching leather-bound volumes, the kind that look good but I can't imagine anyone really reading.

I curled into the deep sofa, sketching my reflection in the

glass windows. My face appeared translucent, as if it could blend into the dim shadows and disappear right through the glass. I tried to draw my blurred image contrasted to the hard edge of the couch. The dark outline of the beach was barely visible beyond the window. All the while I wondered what was going on in the other room. Gradually, the pencil became very heavy in my fingers and I felt myself nodding off.

I must have fallen asleep, because I awakened to the sound of loud, angry voices.

"Lay off, Louie," I heard Jason growl.

"You better listen to me," Louie shouted in the voice she usually saves for my parents, "or you'll be sorry." What were they fighting about?

"You're full of it," came Jason's reply as I dashed out and right smack into him.

"We always seem to be bumping into each other," he said.

"What time is it?" I asked crossly. "And why are you and Louie shouting at each other?"

"She's just having a fit. Totally irrational." Jason shook his head and rolled his eyes to the ceiling.

"Maybe the steak did her in," I retorted.

"I guess you're not going to let me forget the steak. You two sisters sure have a one-track mind."

"What do you mean?" I started to ask, but Jason had maneuvered me into the corner of the hallway. He was standing so close that our bodies were practically touching. I caught my breath. When he leaned over and tried to kiss me, I ducked.

"Cut that out. You're Louie's friend."

"Not at the moment," he said. "Come on, Beth. I think you're cute."

"I think you're awful," I retorted, scooting around him toward the living room. "Louie," I called, "we'd better go home." My first chance at a real kiss and I blew it. A good thing I had my back to Jason, because I could feel my cheeks burning.

Louie was pacing, hands on her hips. "We're already two hours late," I told her. "We'd better call."

"No, let's just go home now." She grabbed her purse.

Jason strolled in as if nothing had happened. "You girls want to stay and take a moonlight swim?"

"Some other time, perhaps," snapped Louie, and stalked out. I was right behind her, but Jason put his hand on my arm and stopped me.

"May I call you, Beth?"

"That's my name," I said.

"I mean on the telephone."

"Me?" I asked in stupid disbelief.

"Shy girls appeal to me," said Jason. "Your sister's too bossy."

"I'm not shy," I said, afraid to meet his eyes.

"Does that mean yes?" I shrugged. "I know I've started off all wrong with you, Beth. But I really do want to know you better. O.K.?"

I nodded and hurried out to the car. Louie was furious.

"What happened?" I asked. "I thought you liked him."

"I'll bet you think he's hot," she said, "but there's a kid with some weird ideas."

"What do you mean?"

"Don't bother me about it. I'll handle Jason my own way."

He likes *me*, I wanted to tell Louie, but I knew she wouldn't believe me. I'd experienced Jason's weirdness at the grocery store. But when I thought about how I felt when his hand touched my arm, I preferred to drop the subject. My mother always says that what you don't know can't hurt you.

Our house was dark when we pulled into the driveway, but the minute we stepped inside, lights started popping on. First I heard Mother's slippers flapping down the hall; then I saw her worried face at the door. Behind Mother was Dad, his eyes blinking to adjust to the light, his face scowling.

"You girls better have a good explanation for this."

"How about a flat tire?" stated Louie calmly. "I'm tired. I'm going to bed. Give Beth the third degree, not me. It's not that late."

"Only one-thirty in the morning," Dad said. "I should have known you'd drag Beth to one of your sleazy parties."

"Oh right, Dad. My parties are sleazy, and poor, innocent Beth is going to be corrupted."

"It wasn't like that, Dad," I said. "We were at a friend's and . . ."

"Go to bed, Beth," Mother said. "We'll handle Louisa."

"Why is this my fault?" Louie protested.

"You shouldn't have been so sarcastic," I hissed. "Now they'll make a big deal."

"This family makes me sick," shouted Louie. "It's always my fault. We ran out of gas, and we had to walk to the nearest station, which was two miles away, and that's the truth. Right, Beth?" She narrowed her eyes and glared at me. This was stupid. Our explanation could have been so simple: we were late because we lost track of the time. No big scene. No need to lie. But Louie expected me to back her up. If I didn't, she'd be furious for days. I hated to go along with her, but it was too late for our parents to accept the real story.

"Yes," I said quietly. "We had a lot of trouble. We're sorry. Can we go to bed now?"

Our parents gave each other helpless looks. We filed out of the living room in opposite directions—my parents to their room down the hall, my sister and I upstairs. Just a few hours ago, Louie and I had been giggling; now I stared past her grimly. We went to bed without speaking.

3

SUNDAY, Louie slept late. She moaned and groaned, tossing and turning in her sleep until I gave up trying to read in bed and went outside to weed the garden with Dad. He takes care of our house as if it were a castle, even though it's a four-room bungalow. People always stop to admire the pink bougainvillea that climbs in thick patches up the front wall. Side by side, we worked in the flower beds, which were filled with petunias, zinnias, and azaleas. I lost myself in the profusion of color and sweet fragrance.

"Your mother couldn't sleep, she was so worried last night," Dad said.

"I guess we should have called," I said, feeling guilty for lying.

"You and Louisa were gone till all hours. And Louisa has used the out-of-gas story too many times for me to believe her."

I concentrated on digging a perfect hole, but I couldn't block my thoughts about Jason. What if he showed up? I imagined him pulling up to the house on his Harley. I'd climb on the seat behind him. About the time he stopped gunning his motor, Mother would start shrieking. I groaned.

"What's the matter?" asked Dad.

"Nothing," I said, yawning. "I'm a little tired." After a while, Mother appeared with a tray of lemonade. The three of us sat on the front porch steps.

"Put Beth in the middle," said Mother.

"Sandwich," my parents bellowed, squeezing me from both sides. "Stop! You're smothering me." It was one of our old standbys.

"Why don't I call Louie to come down?" I suggested. "She's never around when we're having fun."

"Not today," Mother said. "She's in such a bad mood she'd turn fresh milk sour."

"I heard that," cried Louie, appearing at the door. "The three of you love to leave me out, to talk behind my back." She loomed over us, her red hair glowing in the sunlight. From our position on the steps, Louie seemed almost larger than life. Sometimes I think her mere physical presence disturbs my parents, who are both short and plain-looking. It's as if they can't understand how they produced a daughter like Louie, as if she appeared out of nowhere.

Louie stepped down. Her lips quivered. She didn't look so big anymore.

"Mom's just kidding," I told her. "Here, have some lemonade."

"No, thank you. I'm going out." She flounced off. A dramatic exit, as usual. Who could blame her? They treated her like a natural disaster.

"See what I mean," said Mother. "I wish she were more like you." I began to squirm, eager to get off by myself.

"Maybe she'll come to her senses when she goes away to college," said Dad.

"How do you know she wants to go away?" I asked.

"The way she behaves, I'll bet she already has her bags packed," said Mother.

"I think going away to college would be fun," I said.

"You do, do you," said Dad. "Well, we'd miss you too much."

"No, really, I've heard that Florida State has a great art department."

"You still have a couple of years before we have to worry about that," said Dad, clearing his throat, which meant he wasn't going to talk about it anymore.

"But if Louie wants to stay here, can I go?" I persisted.

"But you're such a homebody," said Mother. "I can't see you leaving Sand Key."

"Florida State isn't that far away. Besides, the world doesn't begin and end in Sand Key."

"For us it does," said Dad firmly.

It doesn't for me, I wanted to say, but the stern expression on his face stopped me.

"What's more important right now are your plans for the summer. Have you thought about what you want to do?" asked Dad. "You've never helped in the store very much. About time you gave it a try."

"After all," added Mother, "we're counting on you." She stroked my back possessively, as if I were her pet kitten. "My sweet little Beth." I pulled away. My stomach tightened.

Whenever they bring up the store, I get nervous. Working there is pure torture, especially dealing with customers. I could envision a long, hot summer in the dimly lit store, stammering wrong information and sneezing from the sawdust. Besides, I knew exactly what I wanted to do instead. The poster on the school bulletin board had announced a statewide art competition. Winners would receive a scholarship to a six-week painting workshop at Florida State University, a $150 prize, and art supplies.

"I want to go to summer school," I informed my parents quietly. They exchanged glances.

"What for? Your grades are excellent," Dad said.

"There's a painting course offered at the university."

"It's fine to draw in your spare time," said Mother, "but you can't expect us to pay for lessons."

"Maybe I could get a scholarship."

"Then we'd have to hire extra summer help," said Dad.

"And the university is twenty miles up the beach. How will you get there?" added Mother.

"By bus, of course."

She began twisting the cord on her belt. "You're too young to go all that way on the bus. In the summer, the migrants ride the buses and . . ."

"You let Louie take the bus all the time," I cried.

"That's different." Dad cleared his throat again.

"Mother, will you please think about it? Miss Blues, the art teacher at school, thinks my drawings are good."

"You mean that lady who wears glitter on her hair?" Mother laughed.

"Forget it, Beth," said Dad. "Your place is at the store. Come on, Mother. Let's take a walk." The conversation was closed. When they both agreed, it was impossible to budge them. I knew that art lessons would have to be postponed. Maybe I did owe it to my dad to work at the store. But the thought of spending my time there made me shudder. I went inside and curled up in the closet to sketch, hoping to ease my frustration. I was so busy drawing I didn't answer the phone until the sixth persistent ring.

"Beth," I heard a boy say, "what are you doing?" I dragged the phone inside the closet and practically stuffed myself into a corner on the floor.

"Jason?" I whispered, my cheek pressed to the receiver.

"What's the matter?" he asked. "You sound as if you're chewing on cotton."

"What do you want?"

"I told you I'd like to see your drawings," he said. "Why don't I come by later?" There was a brief lag in conversation while I mulled over the invitation.

"I'll meet you at the corner of Main Street at seven-thirty," I told him.

"Don't forget to bring your sketchbook," he said. "And I've got a book to show you, too."

I agreed and hung up quickly before I lost my nerve. Turning on my back, still clutching the phone, I hugged myself. The phone cord slipped right out of the plug and clattered down the hall. Just like that, I felt good again. Even though my folks thought my artwork was useless, at least someone was interested. And that someone happened to be the handsomest boy I'd ever met. I couldn't wait until I saw him again.

Later that evening I told Mother I was going to meet a friend at the beach. "Don't go near the water or stay on the dock after dark," Mother warned me. "You never know who's lurking out there."

"Oh right," remarked Louie, who was preoccupied with polishing her nails purple, "maybe Jaws or Blackbeard the Pirate."

Mother turned to her and said, "Don't start, Louisa," which gave me the chance to leave before she could ask any questions.

Seven p.m. Soon the sun would go down, and dusk would shield me from curious eyes. It's not a cliché that folks in a small town know everyone else's business.

Sunsets in Sand Key are spectacular. The sky becomes a kaleidoscope of color, and on a humid night, the spectrum

27

of reds to gold vibrates at the edges, translucent and hazy. I sat down on the curb to watch, feeling so full inside that I wanted to reach up and pull the glowing sky toward me. Jason was still a secret, even to me, but the idea of him was warm and bright as the setting sun. I was so preoccupied I was hardly aware of someone calling my name from far away. And then Andy Kohn stood at my side, nudging me out of my reverie.

"I yelled from my window," he said, "but you didn't answer. Why are you sitting all alone with that dopey look on your face and smelling like an overdose of perfume?"

"What if I told you I had a date?"

"You mean with a member of the opposite sex . . . Are you cheating on me?"

"Come on, Andy." I giggled. "Why not? Is that so hard to believe?"

"Well, I don't know. I mean I thought we . . . You usually tell me what you're up to." Andy sounded disappointed.

"I just did." It's not easy to keep secrets in this town, but I was determined to, at least for tonight.

"You know what I mean." Andy was still standing over me, which gave me a good view of his bony ankles and short trousers. I tugged on his cuffs.

"Don't be cranky. So much has happened in the last day, I haven't had a chance."

"Why isn't your date picking you up at the house?" Andy asked suspiciously.

I shrugged. "Listen, do you have to be hanging around like a chaperon when he comes?"

Andy stiffened and scowled down at me. "I can take a hint, but don't think I'm not going to be checking him out from my window." When Andy took off, I decided to go farther down the street to avoid his snooping. Fortunately, it was starting to get dark, the evening shadows lengthening as the sky turned from pink to gray. Close to the beach, I spotted Jason strolling toward me in bathing trunks, a red polo shirt, and an irresistible smile.

"Yeo, babe," he said. "Ready?" Before I could answer, he squeezed my hand and pulled me in the direction of the beach. I saw his motorcycle parked by the boardwalk. Slipping off my sandals at the gate, I dug my toes into the soft, cool sand. There was a slight wind. When I shivered, Jason put his arms around me. He was so tall, I hardly reached his shoulder.

"You're really a lightweight," he said. "I feel as if I should hold on tight to keep you from slipping away." Sometimes being small has its advantages. I glanced at him shyly. Boys at school shove girls around and act goofy. But Jason was completely at ease. "Terrific. No one's on the beach," he said, flinging off his shirt. "Let's go swimming." He splashed into the water, as I stood there remembering my mother's orders not to go near the water. I checked the vicinity for monsters and rapists, but all I could see was Jason waving at me, and I felt absolutely safe and happy. What do I do now, I thought, clutching my notebook and wishing it were a bathing suit. I'd never gone skinny-dipping with a boy and didn't intend to start now. Hesitating at the edge, I dipped my toes in.

"What are you waiting for?" yelled Jason. I laid my notebook on the sand, took two steps farther, and, after pausing dramatically, I strolled in the water with all my clothes on. Jason grinned. "You're quite a sight."

"The water is freezing," I yelled.

"This will get you used to it." A cold spray of water slapped over me. With that, I found myself locked in Jason's arms. I squirmed out of his grasp, and before he could grab me again, I pushed on his head and dunked him.

"You're in for it now," he sputtered. But I somersaulted under the water and quickly swam back to shore, leaving Jason far behind.

"I must be out of practice," he said, emerging from the water a few seconds later. I hardly struggled at all when he swung me up in his arms.

"Don't tell me I'm light as a feather," I said.

"You're hardly a sack of potatoes," he said, depositing me on the sand. He spread some towels and plopped next to me. Why had I ever dreamed of being big? I wrapped the towel around me.

"I don't know many girls like you," Jason said. "You're really refreshing. The girls at school are so aggressive. If you walk into their rooms, they either attack or engage you in some kind of intellectual debate. And they prance around in their underwear."

"Sometimes I wish I were more like those girls you're describing."

"No way, Beth," Jason protested, slipping his arm around my waist. "You're adorable just the way you are. And you swim like a fish!"

"That's me, an adorable little fish." But coming from Jason, it didn't sound so terrible. "What's it like to go to boarding school?" I asked, removing his hand and edging away.

"I'll tell you if you come closer." How could I resist? I inched back. "That's better," he said. We lay side by side, my head resting on his shoulder.

"Go on," I prompted.

"I've been away from home since eighth grade. So far, I've been to three different schools. They were all crummy —glorified concentration camps. My folks are always traveling. They think a kid cramps their style. I don't care. I visit my friends on holidays and do what I want. As long as

they keep my checking account full, I don't need them."
His voice had an edge. I wanted to ask him why he needed
to steal a steak if his parents gave him so much money.

"I was heavily into sports at school. There are three
cliques there: the drudges, who hibernate in the library and
study; the freaks, who party all the time; and the jocks. I
sprained my ankle at the beginning of football season and
had to drop out. So I began hanging around with the freaks.
We thought we were pretty cool, with beer parties and pot
in the rooms, music turned full blast. But last month, we
got busted. The idiot dorm master reported us. Everyone
was high in my room, so I got suspended. The headmaster
used me as an example, announced my name in chapel and
made a big deal out of it. But wait till my parents get home.
They'll make one phone call and I'll be back." He spoke in
a flat voice as if he'd just memorized a speech and was
trying it out. Even though I felt flattered that he'd chosen to
confide in me, his cocky attitude bothered me.

"How can they do that?" I asked.

"My grandfather gave the school a pile of dough. They
wouldn't dare bust me for the year. I'd like to drop out
anyway and stay here." He paused. "Especially now that
I've met you." Suddenly I thought of Louie. What would
she say if she knew I was here with Jason?

"What about Louie?" I said.

"What about her? I know a hundred girls like her,"
Jason said. "But I had a feeling about you right away."

"Yes, but . . ." My feelings about Jason were as confus-
ing as two sets of directions to the same place.

"No buts, Beth." And the way he said my name made
me quiver again. He pulled me closer and nuzzled his lips in
my hair. "You're really something else. You blow me
away."

When we kissed, I was willing to forget the steak, the

Snickers bars, and even what my family might say if they found us together. We rolled onto the sand, but my clothes felt like glue, sticky and gritty. I started squirming. Soon we were tickling each other, giggling. That's when I heard a loud, furious voice coming from the direction of the street.

"Dammit, Jason, where are you? Beth? Beth? Are you two creeps out there?" Louie. It had to be. No one else sounded like a 100-decibel foghorn. What was she doing here? We scrambled up and raced to the boardwalk, still laughing. But when we stood before Louie, who was pacing and sputtering, about to make a scene, we calmed down. Her red hair was disheveled, and her face was contorted with anger.

"What's going on?" she demanded. "Beth, you look ridiculous." She glared at me, at my wet clothes and my legs covered with sand. I wanted to say something, anything, but couldn't.

"We were just taking a walk," Jason said. I waved my sandals as if to prove his point.

"That's not all you were doing. Come on, Beth. Let's get out of here. Now."

"Hold on. Beth's with me," said Jason. "I can take her home."

Louie turned to me. Even in the dark, I could tell she was gloating. We both knew if I went back to the house with Jason my parents would go crazy.

"Thanks anyway, Jason. I'd better do what she says."

"Sure. I'll see you around." He stalked off. I was tempted to murder my sister.

"What's the big idea?"

"Andy called three times to see if you were home yet. Finally, I asked him what his problem was, and he told me you had a date with some guy." She looked proud of herself, as if she'd just cracked a secret code.

32

"So you figured out I was with Jason and came looking for us. Why? You don't even like him."

"You don't know him, Beth. He's trouble."

"You're just jealous. You'd rather see me relegated to the storage closet." I put on my sandals and marched away from her, but she was scrambling behind, yelling at me in her piercing Wanda Witch voice.

"I'm warning you," screamed my sister. But I didn't care. Not only was I soggy and tired, but all I could think about was Jason and the way he made me feel, lying next to him.

4

"I'M NOT MAD at you anymore," announced Louie Monday morning. She stood behind me as I wound my long brown hair into a bun. My first period at school is art class. When I'm working in the studio, I don't like strands of hair straggling in my face. I kept pinning my hair without answering. "Truce," said Louie. She rolled her eyes at me.

"Stop staring like I'm a creature from outer space," I told her. She wouldn't leave me alone until I gave in.

"I just find it amusing that my little sister's growing up."

"You don't look amused," I said. "Anyway, I'll probably never see Jason again after that lovely scene you made last night."

"That would be a lucky break," Louie said. "Someday you'll thank me."

"Lucky for whom? You or me?" I retorted. I was surprised at myself for being so tough with Louie. Usually she makes the wisecracks and I try to remain unfazed.

In the kitchen, Louie told Dad she'd work after school. "I like to help with inventory."

"What about you, Beth?" he asked.

"O.K.," I said, without much enthusiasm. Counting nails wasn't my idea of fun. But when Dad beamed, I was glad I'd agreed.

"You never look as happy when I say I'm coming," complained Louie as she barged out, mad as usual. Her friends were piled in a blue convertible waiting for her. She flashed a brilliant smile and tossed her hair. They sped off without offering me a ride. They never do. I found Andy at the corner, lounging against the streetlight.

"Thanks for mentioning my date to Louie," I told him.

He gave me a sheepish smile. "I got worried. Who is this guy, anyway?"

"It doesn't matter. He's not the type to get too interested in a town girl," I said, hoping to sidetrack him.

There are unspoken rules in Sand Key. The townies and the tourists don't mix except to do business. A girl here got pregnant a few years back. The boy, whose family owned a vacation house, tried to bribe her to have an abortion. She refused. There was a real scandal. It even made the *Sand Key Chronicle*. "Just remember Cassie Sue Kramer," Andy remarked, elbowing us through a crowd of kids in front of the school.

I was glad my first period was pottery, so I could get my mind off Jason. Fashioning a pot on the wheel demands total concentration. One jerky movement and the pot caves in. I love the feel of wet clay spinning through my fingers. It's strange, but the only time I totally concentrate is when I'm making art. My energy is directed—flowing from my mind to my fingertips and onto the material I'm working with. Other skills don't come as easily. My father says that if it's so simple to draw a picture, I should challenge myself to learn something else. But that's not the point. The ease, the feeling of comfort, is only the first step. After learning a technique, one needs to develop a style. Maybe working on an exercise in algebra or building a cabinet requires the same effort, but I'm not good at solving equations or doing woodwork.

One of the few people who understands how I feel is my art teacher. She calls herself Burgundy Blues, but her real name is Beulah Livingston. "If your parents gave you a name like that," she once said, "you'd change it, too." I know how she feels. "I would have preferred Burgundy Soul, but people might have gotten that mixed up with the fish."

She's the closest thing Sand Key has to a punker. Her hair is short cropped, with odd strands sticking up, and it varies in color from pink to orange. She's not into leather or chains, but she loves zebra stripes and big enamel earrings. "I developed my sense of style," she told me, "at the London Academy of Fine Arts." She's such a great teacher that the faculty puts up with her.

Most of the kids think she's bizarre. I did, too, until I started taking her classes. She plays Billie Holiday records as well as Boy George and the Culture Club. "To stimulate your creativity," she says. It works, too. There are rhythms in music that correspond to the vibrations of color on canvas. Listening and absorbing the sounds helps loosen me up.

"Press in lightly right there," Burgundy instructed, "and you'll be able to narrow the neck of the pot." I dipped my fingers in the jar of water and carefully manipulated the clay, but the wheel was turning too fast. Too much pressure on the clay. The top of the pot drooped over and a glob spliced off in my hands.

"Whoops, there goes another one," I said.

Burgundy laughed. "Try it again, Beth. Say, kiddo, have

you thought about submitting a portfolio for the competition at Florida State?''

"Sort of," I admitted. Students were invited to submit ten drawings on the same theme, but I hadn't yet found an interesting subject. And there was also the problem of my parents.

"Well, you still have a few weeks to hand them in. It's up to me to choose our school's applicant to the contest."

Later, I doodled my way through math and social studies, but it wasn't until the bell rang that I realized what I'd been drawing. One profile after another, and they all looked like Jason. He was even taking over my scribbling time!

At three o'clock I raced for the exit. There was a bunch of kids crowded around a car at the end of the walk. Two cheerleaders were perched on the hood. I'm so nearsighted I couldn't tell who it was until I was almost on top of them. Jason! He sat behind the wheel of the Jaguar I'd seen parked in front of his house. Around the car hovered an admiring crowd. I wanted to shrink, to disappear. He'd been discovered. What would he want with me now? But as I ducked around the corner, I heard a loud whooping yell. Barefoot, wearing a pink Izod and madras Bermudas, Jason bounded toward me.

"Beth, Beth. Over here. I've been waiting for you."

I looked around as if he was calling someone else. My heart thumped so loudly I was afraid everyone in Sand Key could hear it.

Jason, smelling of lemon aftershave and tobacco, dressed in his casual preppy clothes, was a vision. And this vision had his arms around me! The cheerleaders, jocks, and hangers-on moved to let us through. Like the Red Sea, the waves parted. They gaped; one of the boys whistled.

Jason opened the door of the car. "Yeo, babe. Your carriage awaits," he said. I climbed inside, feeling like

Cinderella. Would the Jaguar turn into a pumpkin in front of everybody? Out of the corner of my eye I saw Andy skulking by the bushes, regarding me with a puzzled expression. Then Jason and I zoomed down Spruce Drive, toward the Outer Beach Road. I leaned against the leather cushions and closed my eyes. I felt as if I were dreaming.

"Hey, princess," Jason said, "did you think about me?"

5

"I THOUGHT about you," I said. "I think about most things. I didn't leave you out."

"What did your sister say about me the other night after you abandoned me?"

"Nothing much," I said. "Look, I'm really sorry about that. Louie overreacted."

"Well, tell her to mind her own business." He banged his fist on the steering wheel. "She's a real menace. Sometimes I'm grateful to be an only child."

"Louie isn't so bad," I said. "Anyway, thanks for picking me up today."

"Are you glad I did?" He sounded a little uncertain, as if he wasn't sure how I'd react.

"Glad!" I said. "Do bears like honey?"

Jason's face relaxed. He turned up the radio and started singing. His voice was rich and full. "Bye, bye, Miss American Pie. Drove my Chevy to the levee but the levee was dry." He handed me a paper bag. "Here's something you didn't think about. I found it covered with sand." Inside was my notebook.

"In your haste to desert me, you left it on the beach." I laughed.

"This is for you, too." He reached behind the seat and pulled up a book. *French Impressionism at the Louvre.*

"Is this for me?"

"It's my favorite book about painting," he said. "I went to that museum in Paris. Your drawings remind me of some of the pictures I saw there. I marked some pages for you."

"You mean you looked through my sketchbook? What did you think?"

"You're a terrific swimmer," Jason said. Then he paused. "But you're an even better artist." I wondered if my face was beaming, because I felt all lit up inside. "And," he continued, "I'd like to commission you to do my portrait."

"Really?" I held up my school notebook, which contained today's scribbling: Jason's face from every angle. He balanced it on the dashboard. "Wow! Can I have these?"

"If you want. But I can do better. Why don't we go to the beach? You can pose for me." Jason, with his classic profile and wonderful body, would be a perfect subject. Better than Michelangelo's David.

"Maybe later," he said, "but first I'd like to go to that shopping mall near Grand Key Bay. I thought we'd look around and have some dinner. The café serves great rum swizzles."

"We have to stop so I can call the store," I said. "My mother worries if she doesn't know where I am." In the back of my mind, I remembered my promise to Dad this morning.

"My mother doesn't care where I am as long as it's not around her," Jason said. I felt sorry for him. Going to the beach would have been more fun, but I didn't want to disagree. He was on his own, but I suspected he wasn't happy about it. While he concentrated on his driving, I could stare openly. He was beautiful. The urge to run my fingers over his tight, flat stomach was so strong that I had to keep my hands clasped. If you have to be tactile, a little voice inside warned me, stick to making clay pots. There was so much about Jason that made me curious. I wanted to know everything about him—if he rode a tricycle when he was three, if he cried when he skinned his knee, if he had ever been in love. He glanced over and took my hand. The way he grinned, I could tell he knew I'd been staring at him.

"Jason, do you miss your parents?"

"It's hard to miss people you hardly know," he said. "Even when I made All-State at school, they didn't come to the game. They don't pay attention to anything I do. My mother's into being glamorous, running around the world from one party to another. I don't think she wants her jet-set friends to know she's got a seventeen-year-old son. And my father's a real dud. I haven't exchanged a decent word with him in years. He's so uptight, he probably makes love in a dinner jacket." He paused and grinned at me. "What do you wear when you make love?"

I felt my face turning red. I pulled my hand away.

"I was just teasing," he said. "Give me back your hand, princess."

With Jason, I felt like a princess. Louie keeps saying that quiet people are losers who never get what they want. Yet here I was with the sexiest boy in the whole state of Florida. He had chosen me over Louie. Maybe her theory was wrong.

We pulled into one of those new shopping malls with a hundred fancy stores. The parking lot was crawling with Mercedes, Cadillacs, and Rolls-Royces.

"This place is for tourists, not townies," I said.

"Come on, we'll turn you into a tourist. I know just the place."

But I don't care about looking like a tourist, I wanted to tell him. Still, it might be fun to act out a fantasy. Jason's fantasy. He made an adventure out of a simple outing. I followed him into the most exotic shop I'd ever seen. There were live parrots in cages, dozens of tropical plants, racks bulging with gold and silver dresses. Disco music played and lights flickered from a mirror ball revolving on the ceiling. There was an aroma of spicy perfume. The salespeople were very thin. Jason stopped at the jewelry counter. The glass cases were filled with gold necklaces and pearl earrings.

"I need a fabulous gift for my fiancée," announced Jason in a superior tone. "The sky's the limit. Isn't it, princess?" he said, pulling me close. "What a precious little thing," said the saleslady, who, anticipating a big sale, went into immediate action. She fluttered, waving her arms, and twittered like a canary. "Take a look at these trays of rings." Jason was acting strange, his face animated; his voice took on an unreal pitch—slow and seductive.

"Talk to her," he whispered when she bent down to get some more rings. I'd never seen so many rings in one place. Two or three were stuck in every slot on the velvet trays. I saw a ruby ring circled with diamonds. It was the kind of ring I'd seen on ladies at the Sand Key Beach Club. Suddenly I caught on. Jason expected me to divert the saleswoman's attention.

"I'm getting out of here," I whispered to Jason. But as I turned to go, I saw Jason's fingers dart out and curl back like a snake's tongue. A crazy panic seized me. I had visions of being hauled away in Officer Muncie's patrol car. I felt myself bouncing up and down. Just as Jason started another grab, I flipped the tray off the counter out of his reach. "Catch it," cried the saleswoman as the rings clattered under the ledge and across the floor. Jason was so surprised he caught one in midair and actually handed it back to her.

"Sorry," I managed to sputter. While a cluster of salespeople crawled around retrieving the rings, Jason grabbed my arm and dragged me toward the exit.

"I guess I'm not ready to be engaged," I said.

"I'll give you a ring," whispered Jason. "I'll wring your neck."

"How could you pull such a crazy stunt?" he asked in the parking lot.

"What you were doing was even crazier," I answered.

By now I was shaking and my cheeks felt hot. Jason put my hand against his pants pocket. The rings felt like needles pricking my fingers through the material. "That caper wasn't a total waste," he said smugly.

What is wrong with you? I wanted to scream, but I couldn't speak. I found myself getting into his car, closing my eyes, and trying to space out. He drove to a secluded road. Then he pulled out the rings and spread them on the dashboard.

"For you, princess." When he tried to put one on my finger, I pushed his hand away. Here we were all alone on a beach at sunset. The best-looking boy in the world had just tried to give me a gold ring. A perfect picture, except for one small detail. The ring was stolen, and the boy was a possible kleptomaniac.

Staring at him in disbelief and fury, I threw the ring at him. "O.K., O.K., be a little goody-goody, Miss Goodall. Jeez, don't you know the expression 'Never look a gift horse in the mouth'?"

"I'm getting out of this car right now." As I turned the handle, Jason reached over to stop me.

"I just wanted to give you something," he said in a plaintive, little-boy whine.

"I know."

He pulled the gold chain with his St. Christopher's medal off his neck. "Please take this. I swear I didn't steal it. Come on," he said, putting his arm around me. "Don't be angry with me. I swiped a couple of cheap rings. What's the big deal?" I pushed him away. "O.K., O.K., I promise I'll send them back."

"Jason, I don't understand. You don't need to steal things."

"Why are you hanging out with me?" he demanded. I shook my head. "Remember the other night when I told you I had a feeling about us?"

"What was the feeling—that we could be Bonnie and Clyde?"

He took my fingers and closed them around his medal. "Don't give up on me now, princess." I slipped the chain around my neck.

6

I WASN'T LATE for dinner, which was probably the only good outcome of the whole seedy adventure. Mother didn't question where I'd been, even though I'd forgotten to call. She was too upset over Louie, who yelled at my parents through three courses. She started by spearing the still-frozen pizza rolls with her fork.

"I need fifty dollars more for a prom dress."

"The prom's not until January, Louisa," Mother said. "You'll earn enough by then. Besides, what's wrong with last year's dress?"

"All I'm asking for is an advance on my salary. I'll work for it." I was surprised at Louie. She never planned this far in advance. By the time Mother served the main course, rubbery liver and onions, Louie vowed she'd quit school and run away. At dessert (melted ice cream), she threatened suicide. "I'll just kill myself. Then you'll be sorry." Dad picked up his bowl and slurped the liquid, which made Louie even angrier.

"That's right. Ignore me. You think it's all a big joke."

"Louisa," Dad said, "stop carrying on. You have an

45

allowance, and you make $3.50 an hour at the store. It's not our fault that you go over your budget.''

"I need extra money," wheedled Louie, her voice sounding desperate.

"Beth never bothers us about money. Why do you need more than she does?"

"Beth stays home all the time. She doesn't even work. So you're comparing apples to oranges."

"Besides, Beth's younger than you," my mother added in a placating tone.

"I work at home," I protested. "Just because I don't work at the store . . ."

"Speaking of the store, Beth," Dad said, eager to change the subject, "you promised to be there after school today. What happened?"

That's when I felt the St. Christopher's medal around my neck burning as if it were branded on my skin. If my parents noticed, they'd barrage me with questions I knew were impossible for me to answer. "I—I worked late in the art room," I stuttered. "Dad, I'm really sorry." Quickly I ran to our room. Digging through my basket of stones, I hid the necklace at the bottom. My pebbles looked dull and worthless next to the glittering golden charm.

As I pulled out my hand, my fingers grazed an unfamiliar object. I tugged. What emerged through the mosaic of colored glass was a half-empty bottle of Jack Daniels. I felt the skin on my face tighten and a dull throbbing in my head. "Damn her. Damn her." Mother would die if she found out. Just what she needed. One daughter hiding booze, the other running around with a thief. Like an insect, I rolled into a ball on my bed. Stuffing the bottle under one pillow, I pressed another pillow over my head. I didn't hear Louie come in.

"What's your problem?" she said, grabbing the pillow. "Lovers' quarrel? I saw you drive off with Jason today."

"This is my problem," I said, producing the bottle and waving it at her.

"I brought it back from a party last week," Louie said. "It's no big deal."

No big deal. I'd heard that expression from Jason, too. "I'm curious to know what *is* a big deal to you?" I said, trying very hard to sound mature.

"Don't give me that 'holier than thou' voice," Louie retorted. "If Mom and Dad knew what you've been up to, they wouldn't be too thrilled."

I felt my chest tighten. "You're not going to tell them about . . . Jason." I whispered his name.

"If you don't get off my case, I sure will." She let out a stream of invectives that ended with "Get out." I was afraid to say, "This is my room, too." At that point, I heard a loud commotion coming from the street. It sounded like a thousand dogs yapping. I opened the window and stuck my head out. There was Andy with six poodles in tow.

"Do your thing," he yelled. They barked and jumped on him. I turned back to face Louie.

"All right, I'm going. But promise . . ." She pursed her lips and pointed to the door. Louie can be as stubborn as our parents.

I went downstairs to find Andy. Sooner or later we'd have to discuss Jason. But what could I tell him? That I was involved with a jewel thief? Andy would probably set all six dogs on me.

"How's the famous poodle doodler?" I asked.

"One more day with these monsters and I might turn to a life of crime." The way Andy was looking at me made me think he had read my mind.

47

"What do you mean?" I said, feeling defensive. Was Andy hinting around about Jason?

"Nothing really," he said innocently. "I just figured anything, even illegal activity, would be better than this." He pointed at the poodles, who slobbered at his feet. "However, you know what they say?"

"No, what do they say?"

"Crime," Andy announced in a deep voice, "doesn't pay." We both laughed.

"That's for sure," I said. "I remember once, when I was five, I grabbed a package of gum at the drugstore. As soon as Mother saw what I was clutching in my grubby paw, she made me take it back. I remember how embarrassed I was. I had to tell the manager I was sorry, that I'd never do it again." I cringed at the memory.

"Well, you never did it again, did you?"

"I guess not. But what if I hadn't been caught?"

"That kind of stuff always catches up with you. I stole two packets of watermelon seeds once. Pulled them off a rack in front of five people. I planted all hundred seeds in the back yard. Spent weeks watering them. I was going to set up a fruit stand on State Highway 105 and sell them to tourists."

"That's real cute, Andy." I smirked.

"Now wait a minute. Here's the best part of the story. Not one seed grew. Not even a tiny sprout. I figured that was my punishment. Poetic justice and all that rot." He paused and peered at me.

"I've been doing some checking. Your new friend is bad news." So my suspicions were correct. Andy knew something about Jason. But I was determined not to let him intimidate me.

"I'll be the judge of that," I said stiffly.

"Apparently he's living all by himself in one of those mansions on the outer road. He charges things all over town without paying his bills . . ."

"But his parents are rich. They'll come down here and take care of things," I protested, as if that excused Jason's behavior.

"That guy's not your type," insisted Andy. "He starts fights and throws his weight around." The dogs were sniffing my feet and tumbling over one another.

"You don't know my type." Andy looked down miserably. I was immediately sorry. "Come on. Give me those leashes. I'll help you walk the dogs."

We trudged down Elm Street in silence. Finally I said, "Andy, Jason's one of those guys that all the girls have crushes on. For some reason, he likes me."

"You act as if he's doing you a favor," said Andy. "It's the other way around."

"You're just prejudiced," I said.

"Maybe. But I don't get it. What is it about the guy besides good old sex appeal?" Andy shook his head.

"He's interesting. Jason's been all over the world. He likes to talk about art, and he even wants me to paint his portrait."

"Oh boy, I've heard that old line before," said Andy.

"You don't want to believe him," I said. "Besides, if he has problems, maybe I can help."

"Don't count on it, Beth," said Andy. "That kid's headed for deep trouble. I don't want you to get mixed up with him."

"Trust me," I said. "I know what I'm doing." Where had I heard those words before? I had about as much control over Jason as my parents had over Louie.

"I'm not sure if you have illusions of grandeur," said

Andy, "or if you're just deluded." Before I could reply, Andy snatched the leashes and the poodles dragged him away into the gray dusk.

I found a DO NOT DISTURB sign on the bedroom door and Louie in bed. My brain was reeling with angry thoughts, all directed toward my sister, who lay face to the wall, pretending to be asleep. Pressing my fingers to my throbbing head, I sat there and listed all my gripes against her. First of all, why did she have to pester Mom and Dad about money at such a bad time? And then there was that bottle hidden in my stone collection. But the thing that bothered me most was the power she had over me now. If she told Mom and Dad about Jason, my romance didn't have a chance. I resisted the urge to smother her with my pillow and decided to try a peaceful approach. In our social-studies class, we learned that diplomacy was one of the best ways to solve world problems. However, if arbitration wasn't working in the Middle East, what made me think I could negotiate with Louie? Nevertheless, I decided to give it a try. "Are you sleeping?" I whispered. No answer. "Louie, I need to talk to you."

"If you're about to give me a lecture on my despicable character and rotten attitude, don't bother," came Louie's muffled retort.

I clenched my fists and said sweetly, "If you really need a new dress, maybe I can help you make it."

Louie let out a loud chortle. "You don't believe for one minute that I want the money for a new dress, do you?"

"No," I admitted, "but whatever you're up to, it must be important. It's not like you to cause so much friction at the dinner table." This note of sarcasm was difficult to contain. For a person who hardly ever loses her temper, I was working up to an explosion. My sister jerked to a sitting position and flipped on the lights.

"You're not fooling me for a minute, Beth. Why don't you get to the point of this stupid conversation?"

"The point is that I don't understand why you have to be so selfish. You don't think of anybody but yourself, and I'm sick and tired of it."

"If things don't improve around here," said my sister in a low voice, "you won't have to worry about me causing trouble anymore."

"What do you mean?"

"I feel horrible around this house. It gets worse and worse."

"Where would you go?" I asked, beginning to suspect what she needed the money for.

"I don't know," said Louie. "Sometimes I get so frustrated I want to burst. Then I try to figure out ways to get away from here, to escape."

"You'll end up traipsing around the world," I told her. "And I'm not allowed to ride a bus to the next town by myself." I scrambled over to her bed and crawled in between the sheets, the way I used to when we were little. "Please stop thinking about running away, Louie," I said. "What would I do without you?" She was shaking under the covers so I squeezed her hand until she calmed down.

"Can you picture Dad's face if he ever caught you riding on the back of a Harley?" Louie said after a while.

"Don't torture me," I groaned, which made her break out laughing. My sister's serious moods are definitely short-lived. "I'm glad you find me so amusing."

"Don't worry, squirt. I won't tell on you."

Pretty soon I could hear the steady breathing of Louie in her sleep. For a long time, I lay there next to her worrying —about this summer, about Jason, about Louie and my parents. Devising a plan for nuclear disarmament seemed an easier problem to solve.

7

THERE ARE TWO expressions Mother uses when Louie gives Dad trouble. "You're treading on thin ice," she says, or "Watch your step." In the last week since she threatened to run away, Louie had been watching her step. She'd been keeping to herself, making notes on a yellow legal pad, and looking mysterious. But when she bounced on my bed and pulled back the covers in the middle of the night, I was afraid her days of good behavior were over.

"Wake up," she rasped. I moaned and flopped over. "Have you gone berserk?"

"Come on, Beth, we have to get going."

"What do you mean?" I forced myself to sit up. There was Louie, fully dressed, regarding me with an expression I'd learned to dread. It was a cross between a devious grin and a sneer, and usually preceded some sort of outrageous act. It was the same face she used before she skipped school or sneaked out the window for a late date. Even if I didn't participate, I always felt implicated.

"Don't you know what today is?"

I shook my head. "Same old reliable Tuesday, as far as

I'm concerned. Louie, even the roosters haven't started crowing yet."

"There aren't any roosters in Sand Key, just seagulls," she retorted.

"What's going on?"

"It's Mom and Dad's twentieth anniversary, squirt."

"Oh no! I completely forgot." I lay down and pulled the sheet over my head. "That's what happens when you fall in love," said Louie. "Premature senility." I groaned. "Well, I've planned a surprise and I need your help."

"What kind of surprise?" What devious scheme had she contrived this time?

"Just look!" She unrolled a long piece of paper. Once I managed to focus, I saw she'd drawn a floor plan of the store. The proportions were clumsy, the perspectives out of whack. Still, the whole effect was impressive. "I'm a lousy artist, but you get the picture." On closer inspection, I saw she'd worked out a complex diagram, redistributing all the merchandise in the store. "Things are too jumbled up in there," Louie stated, sounding very businesslike and sure of herself, "but the folks are always too busy to sort out their stock. One day hammers and nails are dumped on shelf B; the next week they turn up on the other side of the store. Even our regular customers are confused. Yesterday I found mops and brooms under the nail counter. The way I see it, if we work fast, we can give the place a new image."

"How?" I asked, picturing the musty, cluttered old store that hadn't been redecorated in years.

"The store needs to be modernized," she went on, ignoring my question. "This is only the beginning. Mom and Dad will love it. They're always saying we have to get organized." She yanked me up. "Only two and a half hours before the store opens. I can't wait to see their faces when they discover what we've done."

Louie's face was flushed with excitement, but something about her idea bothered me.

"The smell of birdseed makes me sneeze," I told her.

"Quit stalling. We don't have a lot of time." She was so determined I decided to push back my doubts. Maybe Mom and Dad would be pleased by Louie's ingenuity and my contribution.

After I pulled on some old jeans and a work shirt, Louie and I ran down the dark street toward the store. "If we get some of your friends to help," I suggested, "I'll bet we could get everything done by nine." The way Louie curled her lip and shrugged, I realized she couldn't count on them. Her crowd might make fun of her. It wasn't considered cool to participate in an activity so blatantly designed to please one's parents.

"Let's stop at Andy's," I suggested. "I know he'll help."

"O.K., but make it snappy. I'll see you at the store in five minutes."

To wake up Andy, I practically had to break his bedroom window. "Despite the ungodly hour," he said, rubbing his eyes after I explained what I wanted, "this escapade intrigues me. Besides, you might need moral support. Louie is weirder than my mother."

When we walked into the store, Louie had arranged brightly colored poster paints, brushes, and rectangular Plexiglas signs on the floor. "Beth, letter these signs to indicate new sections." She took one look at Andy's pants, which, as usual, were above his ankles, and cracked up. "Why do you always dress like you're ready for a flood?"

Andy regarded Louie with her diagrams and lists and said, "I'm prepared for any major catastrophe." Then she instructed him to lug boxes. Soon we were sorting, stacking, reshuffling cans, cartons, nuts, bolts, tools, pails, and other miscellaneous items into areas designated HOUSE-WARES, GARDEN EQUIPMENT, CLEANING FLUIDS, and PAINT SUPPLIES. The more stuff we moved, the more things seemed to pile up.

Andy said, "How can you ever remember what's what here? I mean, look at these labels—cant hook, nippers, stump spud, and bib washers."

"It's a different language," I called over to him.

"Greek to me," Andy said.

"Not to me," said Louie. "I can tell you what everything stands for."

"What's that, then?" challenged Andy, pointing to the ceiling, where loops of black rubber bands hung like snakes from the rafters.

"Fan belts for car motors and washing machines," Louie said. Andy whistled admiringly and followed Louie downstairs to the basement, where Dad stores backup items as well as the huge trash barrels and rolls of chicken wire that take up too much room upstairs. After they were down there for a while, I started to resent being stuck upstairs all alone. Andy's loud chortling didn't help. He seemed fascinated by Louie, which made me uneasy. That old feeling came over me—all Louie needed to do was snap her fingers and even Andy would drop me for her.

"What's so funny?" I yelled. More gales of laughter. They emerged covered with spiderwebs and dust.

"A dungeon. It's a dungeon down there, coal bin and all," Andy said. I shot him a dirty look.

"Here, Andy," Louie said, pointing to some burlap sacks. "Pull the grass seed into the corner of the garden section. People trip because these bags block the aisles."

Finally we hung the signs and stood back to observe the results of our labors. Toilet plungers were lined straight as a formation of soldiers; the rows of shovels, rakes, and pitchforks stood proud and tall as an army ready for combat. The pipe ripples gleamed in their cubby holes, cunning circles of silver and bronze, like ammunition waiting to be used. Organized as a general, Louie had pasted typewritten labels on the built-in wooden boxes that stored nails, brackets, or knobs. Yet the place, still strewn with merchandise, had a jumbled quality, the jammed-up, shoddy, hit-or-miss disarray of a battlefield. I thought of shipwrecks and salvage lots.

"We've hardly made a dent," Louie groaned. "The next step is to repaint, put in good lighting, and install a new linoleum floor." Undaunted, she scribbled in her notebook. "We've done the best we can this go-round."

Then I realized what was bothering me. Twice a year, Mother sweeps through our bedroom with her plastic bags, broom, and dust cloth, poking around in our drawers, under beds and in closets, pitching everything in sight. A stack of my drawings, Louie's love letters from an old boyfriend, faded-just-right Levi's, and our tattered doll collection disappeared in one fell swoop. No matter how loud we yell, Mother will come tramping through, wreaking havoc whenever the mood strikes her. Will they feel the same way about Louie and me poking around in their territory? My stomach started to tighten. Maybe Louie wanted to start trouble; maybe this was another ploy to prove how tough and independent she was.

At that moment, Dad and Mother burst through the front door. "What's the place doing unlocked?" he was saying to her in a loud, worried voice. Then he saw Louie, Andy, and me standing there grinning.

"What in heaven's name?" sputtered Mother. "What are you kids doing here?" That's when I started getting a sinking feeling. Their faces registered alarm rather than pleasure.

"Look around," said Louie, still cocky. "We've done a little redecorating."

Dad gave Mother a bewildered glance and stared up and down at the signs gleaming in their newly painted colors, at the neat rows of brooms and mops, at the cleared aisles and reorganized shelves, and then at Louie, who was still smiling but tugging at her ponytail nervously. Dad pulled off his cap. "Well, I'll be."

"Here," Louie said, "is a list of all the improvements that still need to be made . . ."

"Where's the cash register?" Mother asked.

"Over there. I moved the checkout counter to that corner so you can have a display case in the center aisle."

"Louisa, I hardly know what to say," Dad said slowly. "You certainly took on a lot of responsibility without checking with us first."

"It's a surprise for your anniversary," I said.

"Yeah, happy anniversary, Mr. and Mrs. Goodall," Andy offered.

"Where are the ladders?" said Mother. "And garbage cans? I can't find my bulletin board." Mother's the type who has to be in charge or she feels disoriented. Right now she wasn't upset with Louie, just confused.

"The whole store was one big chaotic mess," Louie said, her voice shrill.

"Now hold on, Louisa, there's an order to our disorder. Right, Mother?"

"Of course, I knew where everything was," Mother replied.

"Nobody else did," Louie said in a stony voice, "especially the customers."

I grabbed Dad's elbow. "We've been here since six-thirty. We've straightened the whole store. And Louie even has a floor plan." Then I felt a tickle in my nose that erupted into a loud sneeze, and soon I was bent over wheezing from the dust, the grass seed, and plain old nervousness. Everyone started patting me on the back and offering Kleenex except Louie, who stood back and commented, "Just like you, Beth, to create a diversion and get all the attention." She always takes her frustrations out on me, but this time I couldn't blame her for being upset.

"Louie," said Mother, "how could you pull Beth and her friend into this silliness? You know Dad and I have our own ideas about the store. It'll take us days to reorient ourselves."

Louie's face turned pale, rigid with anger and defeat. And I realized my suspicion that Louie was up to no good was unfounded. I wanted to say something, to make more of an effort to defend Louie, but every time they have a big fight, I get nervous and say something silly.

"Oh, hell," she said, "I give up. I'll never please you." Furiously she grabbed her knapsack. Chin raised defiantly, my sister stalked out, kicking a bag of birdseed that was in her path. It ripped and poured over the newly swept floor.

8

AFTER THE FIASCO at the store, Louie and my parents had a major fight. At breakfast the next morning, she announced, "I'm not coming back to work. At least not at your store." She emphasized "your" as if it were a dirty word. Sometimes I think family meals should be declared a national safety hazard. I rolled my eyes to the ceiling and waited for the explosion. Silence. Mother began slicing the English muffins as if she were chopping logs. Dad cleared his throat.

"Do you have an alternative?" he asked slowly.

"Based on my experience," Louie said stiffly, "I'm sure Ace Hardware in the mall will give me a job."

"Well, if that's what you want, Louie," said Mother sweetly.

Louie jerked back in surprise. "I'm sure Beth will fill in for you nicely," added Dad. And suddenly I realized that Louie expected them to beg her to stay. But my parents were actually relieved to be getting rid of her. And for whom? The most inept person in all of southern Florida.

"You must be kidding, Louie," I appealed to her.

"I'm sure Louisa will be quite happy at Ace's," said Dad. Louie stood up, a wooden expression on her face. For once my sister left the room without banging her way out. I'll never forget the look of shame and misery on her face. But my parents were oblivious. Pushing back my chair, I followed Louie outside, where I found her slumped on the grass crying the way she does everything—furiously, intensely, totally self-absorbed. There was nothing I could do to comfort her. Nothing. I felt tears well up in my eyes. No turning back now. It was settled. Mom and Dad decided to draft me as Louie's replacement. She would be on her own, and I was cast again in a part I didn't want to play.

Thanksgiving vacation was about as festive as a wake. Three miserable afternoons, despite my weak protests, I worked at the store, where I fit in about as well as a square peg in a round hole. I found myself hiding at the end of the last aisle, pretending to straighten shelves, but what I was really thinking about had nothing to do with tools, nuts, and bolts.

Whenever I could, I sneaked downstairs to the basement to draw. Over and over I kept repeating, "Someday, when I run off to SoHo," and tried to convince myself that a miracle would happen. My only consolation were the hours spent with Jason, who loved to look at my work, especially the pictures I made of him.

Louie came home late every night and went right to sleep. If I asked her about her new job, she wouldn't answer. When I told her mine was the pits, she stared at me vacantly, as if to say, "So what! It doesn't matter." I preferred the old Louie, cranky but never indifferent.

Finally Monday morning rolled around. I've never been more thrilled to go back to school. I was wandering around the library when Burgundy Blues, resplendent in fuchsia stockings and pink hair sparkling with silver and standing on end, cornered me.

I'd just checked out *Lust for Life*, a biography of Vincent Van Gogh. The artists in Paris around the turn of the century fascinate me. Van Gogh cut off his ear. Gauguin ran away to Tahiti. Picasso loved bullfights and wild women. They lived impetuously while I hid out, drawing pictures in my storage closet the way Emily Dickinson wrote poems in her attic.

Burgundy gave off a heady aroma of gardenia perfume. I didn't even have to turn around to know she was there.

"Beth, I'm still waiting for your drawings. I know you could win a scholarship this summer."

"I don't think so. It takes a portfolio, and I don't have enough really terrific pictures."

"Are you afraid to try?" she goaded gently. "I think you're good enough. What's the problem?"

"It's just that my parents need me to work at the store," I said, deciding to be frank. "They don't like the idea of their daughter being an artist."

"I wager they'll change their minds if you're offered a place in the class."

"Maybe," I said doubtfully. She glanced at my book. "Van Gogh. His paintings are wonderful. So passionate and intense."

"So was his life," I added.

"Beth, not all artists live such dramatic lives. It's a romantic notion we have that artists are outcasts on the edge of society. Most artists, especially women, struggle with problems other than insanity and decadent lives."

"What do you mean?" I wondered what she was getting at. I loved the idea of living on the fringes, imagining myself leading a bohemian life.

"Many women artists struggle with the same problems

you have. Their families don't approve, or take their work seriously. There's a wonderful biography of Mary Cassatt, an American artist who moved to Paris to get away from her strict Philadelphia upbringing. Even Degas used to tell her she was a pretty good draughtsman for a woman.''

"I know her work. You have a poster of a mother and child in your office.''

"Exactly. She chose to paint a very feminine subject but presented it without sentimentality. She was a genius, but people rarely acknowledged that, because she was a woman. Come down to my office, and I'll lend the book to you. And, Beth, reconsider the summer program.'' She enveloped me in a warm hug, glitter from her hair splattering my shirt, and then she disappeared behind the stacks.

I wasn't fooling Miss Blues. She knew how badly I wanted to take that course. What could be better than painting all morning and being with Jason all afternoon. I once read an article about Freud, who talked about the importance of love and work. But I wonder how many people can balance the two. My parents love their work, and they love each other. But their idea of work is not the same as mine.

When Jason met me after school, I decided to combine love and work and asked him again to pose for me.

"Why not.'' He took my books and put his arm around my waist. "You know something, princess? I thought about you all day.''

I wrinkled my nose and raised my eyebrows. "I'll bet. You're so tan. You've probably been playing on the beach. Oh, the life of the idle rich!''

"There's my cycle,'' he said, pointing to the mechanical beast looming ominously across the street. "How about a spin?''

"Not me. Let's walk to the beach.''

"Come on. Just put your feet on the sideboards and your arms around my waist." He hoisted me onto the seat. The next thing I knew, I was behind Jason, holding on for dear life. I had a sense of being lifted and carried away. With the wind blowing my hair in my face, I pressed my body against Jason's back and let myself relax. Streets, houses, billboards blended into one continuous field painting. There was the motor's roar, the pulsating speed, and Jason. At that moment, nothing else in the world mattered. I wanted the ride to last forever.

When he finally stopped, I nearly fell off. "You're trembling," he said. He kissed my hair, my eyes, and my face. "You held on so hard I thought my ribs would crack."

"That was half the fun," I said as I scanned the beach for a good spot to work. Not too far from the shoreline a jagged clump of rocks formed a natural shelter and some shade. "Let's go over there." Jason bounded ahead of me. He grabbed a stick and began writing in the sand.

Quiet! Genius at Work.

Sitting on the sand, making sketch after sketch of Jason, was one of the most satisfying times of my life. He was a terrible model—couldn't sit still. "How about if I take everything off?" he teased, starting to pull down his shorts.

I laughed. "Just be quiet and don't move." He started shifting positions and trying to tease me into taking a swim. I quickly made some thirty-second studies with one continuous line until I almost filled the sketch pad.

He wasn't self-conscious, only restless. After an hour, he'd had it. So, per usual, I followed him into the water with all my clothes on. "You're beautiful," he whispered. You're the beautiful one, I wanted to say, but nobody struts around practically stark naked the way Jason does without already knowing it. We thrashed in the waves, slipping and sliding like two baby porpoises. Jason kissed me so many

63

times my lips felt sore. But when he tried to pull off my shirt, I pushed him away.

"Relax, princess. Don't be so uptight." Diving underwater, I swam to the surface and back to the shore. When Jason emerged, his hair was plastered on his forehead, a grin on his face. "Come here, princess," he said. I went to him and we hugged. "You don't have to be shy with me."

"I know," I whispered, my face pressed to his chest. "I'm just not ready."

"I'll arrange fireworks and a parade when you are," he said.

We drove back to Sand Key just as the sun was going down. At this time of year, the sun is a huge, fiery red ball. It disappears into the ocean, suddenly dropping out of sight. Slowly the sky turns pearl-gray. I thought if I had my pastels I could have almost gotten it right. I've tried to draw a sunset many times, but this evening I had an extra level of consciousness— a special awareness I'd never had before.

When Jason dropped me off at the corner a block away from my house, he said, "I'll see you tomorrow. It's my turn to plan the afternoon."

"You could never beat today," I said.

"You never know, princess." He winked, ruffled my already disheveled hair, and sped off.

9

BRIGHT AND EARLY the next morning I knocked on Burgundy Blues's door. I couldn't wait to show her my drawings of Jason. "Enter at your own risk," came an exasperated voice. I found her bent over her desk, surrounded by folders, out of which various crumpled papers emerged. When she saw me, she brightened.

"I'm inundated with paper work," moaned Miss Blues. She was wearing white overalls, splattered with bright-colored paint. "Please give me an excuse to shove it all aside for a few minutes. This administration is obsessed with keeping records, an exercise I detest."

"Look," I said, placing the sketchbook on her desk. She flipped through the pages, studying them one by one. I watched her face for a reaction.

"These are well done, Beth," she said finally. "But I would call them works in progress. I think you need to go further."

"I don't understand," I said, feeling let down. The sketches were the best I'd ever done.

"What you have here are quick studies. They project one particular mood and a basic pose. What they lack is variety."

"You mean my drawings all look alike?" I was crushed. I'd expected her to be ecstatic.

"Almost," she said. We both peered down at Jason, immortalized in Greek-god splendor. Now the sketches seemed boring and amateurish. "On the other hand," Miss Blues said, "there's a freedom and facility of line here that's quite remarkable."

My spirits started to lift. "Really?"

"Absolutely. Go back and develop the images with a wider range of emotion. Maybe," she mused, "you need some distance from the subject."

"Right now," I groaned, "it's impossible to get some distance from the subject."

Miss Blues tilted her chair back and laughed. "I think I understand your predicament. Well, leave the notebook here. I may submit it to the competition, anyway. The work is good, but you can do even better."

"Maybe I should get Jason to pose for me again," I suggested.

"You'll figure it out. Both Love and Art can take unexpected turns." Miss Blues sighed mysteriously and went back to her papers. I left the art room wondering what she was talking about. Yet it was obvious she knew what I'd been up to.

There didn't seem to be anyone in Sand Key, except my parents, who failed to notice my romance with Jason Teasdale III. Instant celebrity. The boys at Sandstone High regarded me with new eyes. I could no longer move through the halls in blessed anonymity. I was surrounded by curiosity seekers. "What's Jason really like?" (A question

I still couldn't answer.) "Bring him to the bonfire Saturday night?" "He's hot. Aren't you the lucky one!" My sister's friends even offered me a ride to school. The only person who wasn't impressed was Andy. In fact, he made gloomy predictions about my fate, as if I'd committed some unpardonable sin, as if Jason were really a vampire disguised in preppy clothes.

"I'm still the same person. Be happy for me," I pleaded.

"I'll try," retorted Andy in a grumpy voice. We sat on the steps during our free hour. "But I think you've slipped a gear. Every time I see you zooming around town on the back of a motorcycle, clutching that Hell's Angel, I feel like barfing." Then he held his stomach and pretended to gag. I couldn't help laughing. I knew Andy would be my friend no matter what.

"Just call this an experiment in the life of the underworld," I said in an ominous tone.

"Seriously, Beth, that guy may be doing a number on you. I don't want you to get hurt."

"Louie said the same thing. You're both wrong."

"For once you ought to listen to your sister." The bell rang for my fifth-hour class. Speech. It's the only course Louie and I take together. It was her turn to give an oral report. She was crouched in the back row trying to look invisible. I knew she hadn't prepared. Lately she'd been behaving more dopey than usual. When Mr. Higgenbothem called her name, she started shuffling her books as if she couldn't find her paper.

"Forget about notes, Louisa," he ordered. "You should know the material well enough to do without notes."

Louie wobbled like a wooden puppet. She pulled up her shoulders and saluted him. "Yes sir, Mr. Higgenbothem. Front and center." As she stumbled down the aisle, I realized Louie had to be drunk. Rumor had it that some of the kids were sneaking flasks into school. "Please don't make a fool of yourself," I prayed. She tottered against the desk and gazed distractedly around the room. I tried to catch her eye, but she wasn't focusing.

"Go on, Louisa. We haven't got all day," said Higgenbothem.

Louie sighed as if to say, "Well, here goes nothing."

"Sex education," she began in a slightly mushy voice, "is a controversial subject." A few titters broke out, which may have been due to the topic. Still, she managed a coherent opening statement. In the middle of the second sentence, she stopped. "Allen Toft, stop staring at my tits." The class broke up. Louie, encouraged by the laughter, blathered on unintelligibly for a few minutes. She was attempting to describe the classic cartoon on the reproductive system. "First they show you this wriggly line," she said; "that's supposed to be the sperm." She rolled her eyes. "Then the little critters swim upstream." This remark was accompanied by some frantic arm movements. When she decided to grind her hips like a belly dancer, I knew it was all over. By now the class was practically rolling in the aisles. I had slipped down so far in my seat that I felt a crick in my neck.

"That's enough, Louisa. Go sit down," screamed Higgenbothem. Louie turned on him, her voice shrill. "This is a dumb course. I can't stand it."

Higgenbothem grabbed Louie by the shoulder. Every nerve in my body tingled. I couldn't move and I couldn't speak.

"Louisa Goodall, you're a disgrace. Let's go down to the principal's office. Now!" Attempting some semblance of dignity, Louie shrugged him away. "I can manage quite well on my own." She swerved out, followed by Higgenbothem, and me right behind them.

When she made a detour into the ladies' room, I said, "Give me a minute with her, Mr. Higgenbothem. Please?" Without waiting for a reply, I darted past him through the door to find Louie bent over the sink splashing cold water on her face.

"Now you've really had it, Louie. They'll call Mom and Dad. It will be all over the school in an hour." She swung around and lashed out at me. "Is that all you care about? That the whole school will talk about me? Half the school drinks. What do you think we do during lunch hour? Sit around sipping tea and discussing Plato? Wise up. No one gives a damn. Especially not our precious parents. They're too busy trying to sell nuts and bolts."

With that, she straightened up, rearranged her clothes, sprayed some Binaca on her tongue, and marched back out.

"Shall we?" I heard her say to Higgenbothem with such aplomb that I began to suspect that her exaggerated drunkenness was mostly an act. How else could she have recovered in record time?

Fifteen minutes later she emerged from the principal's office, grinning triumphantly.

"Two Wednesday-afternoon detentions," she announced. "That's it!"

We stood staring at each other from opposite ends of the reception room, like two sides of an argument. Then she was swept away by her friends, who gathered outside the door.

In some deep, inexplicable way, I wished Louie had been caught. It wasn't just her arrogance that made me angry. In my mind I could see the faces of the kids in the class leering at her, their expressions almost ghoulish. She was a spectacle to them—like a dancing bear, and she didn't realize it. All my life I'd envied Louie, tagged after her hoping some of her gutsiness would rub off. What my parents had termed "bad character" I called "free spirit." But it wasn't her "free spirit" getting her into trouble.

10

AFTER THE BELL rang, I waited outside for Louie. It was a hundred degrees in the shade, with no breeze. Hordes of kids swarmed down the steps eager to hit the beach or Dairy Queen. Scuffling and shoving, throwing books and jackets, Louie's group rushed past without acknowledging me. But I didn't spot Louie. The street was a tangle of bicycles, cars, and pushing kids, who all shouted at once. Within ten minutes the whole area cleared, except for me sitting forlornly on the steps and imagining my sister passed out on the floor of a broom closet. A few teachers emerged and glanced at me curiously. But I was afraid to ask them if they'd seen Louie. Finally discouraged, I headed home.

There I found her, snoring face down on the living-room floor, her russet hair streaming over her face, her clothes rumpled. Despite the cool image she tried to project, Louie knew as much about drinking as I did. She and her friends had beer parties on the beach, but I'd never seen her come home in bad shape before. I looked closely at my big sister, who in this deep sleep appeared so innocent, so sweet, and I realized that she was as much exhausted from work and too many late nights as she was drunk from her lunch-hour binge. She'd fallen apart today for more than one reason. "Oh, Louie," I whispered to her, "please don't do this to yourself again." Her lips quivered a little. She sighed and rolled on her side. "Rrrumm," she muttered. I wondered what Louie was dreaming, if she'd awaken contrite, or furious with me and the whole world. But I couldn't leave her wiped out on the floor. My parents were due home any minute. I nudged her with my foot. "Rrrumm," she murmured again, and rolled over.

"Upsy-daisy," I said, bending down to pull her to a sitting position. She slumped back, bumping the floor like a rubber tire.

"What an interesting sight," came a voice from the door. "What's the juvenile delinquent done now?" There was Andy, two poodles at his feet, observing us. "Is she wasted?"

"Just in time to help me lug Louie to bed. I'll explain later. Wake up, Louie," I pleaded. "We don't have much time." She wasn't about to budge on her own. Shadows on the wall indicated that five o'clock was rapidly approaching.

"There's only one solution," declared Andy. He dropped the leashes, and the poodles bounded across the room and began licking Louie's face and tugging at the bow in her hair.

"What's going on?" she mumbled, swatting the dogs as if they were flies. They yipped and yapped around her until she bolted up with a start.

"Easy does it," I said. We hoisted Louie to her feet, dragging her in the direction of the bedroom. She flapped her hands and protested.

"Leave me be, you two maniacs." Upstairs she keeled

over on the bed, her left leg dangling down. Grabbing my blanket, I covered her and brushed the hair off her face. I knew she wouldn't want anyone to see her in this condition, but without Andy and his canine rescue team, she'd probably still be on the living-room rug.

"Whew, that was a close call. Thanks, Andy."

"Your life is getting more and more puzzling," he declared, shaking his head as he grabbed the poodles under each arm and thumped down the stairs. At that moment, the doorbell rang.

"What now?" I moaned.

"I'll get it," said Andy.

Outside, lounging against the door frame, stood Jason Teasdale III.

"It's Simon Legree," said Andy under his breath. Of all times for Jason to show up!

"I've got to get rid of him," I whispered.

"That's the best news I've heard all day," Andy said.

"I'm Jason Teasdale." Jason offered his hand to Andy, who regarded it as if it were a grenade.

"Want to play kickball?" Andy said, clearly being perverse.

"Who's this space cadet?" Jason asked.

"Andy Kohn, meet Jason Teasdale." They nodded warily.

"So," I said brightly, "why don't we take a walk? I need some exercise." I marched out the door, but no one followed.

"What's going on, princess?" Jason asked.

"He calls you 'princess'?" Andy said disgustedly. I could tell this wasn't going to work. At that point, I spotted my parents' old Chevy chugging toward us. "Think fast," I cried to no one in particular. The poodles jumped on Jason, drooling and yelping.

"These worthless dogs yours?" he asked Andy.

"Not exactly." Andy hated to admit what he was doing with them, which gave me a terrific but fiendish idea. I threw Andy a meaningful glance. Translated, it meant, "Help me or else." Then I bent down, pretending to pull the poodles off Jason, but unhooking the leashes instead. The dogs, delighted to be free, went scrambling over each other through the door. I knew they wouldn't go far, but Andy, totally neurotic, would imagine the worst.

"Maybe you'd better help him," I suggested to Jason, who burst out laughing as Andy, shirttails flapping, dashed after the dogs.

"I came over to see you, not to chase two swarmy little mutts for that cretin."

"Andy's not a cretin," I retorted. "He'll be in trouble if he doesn't catch them." Our car swerved into the driveway. I could see my parents' faces registering their surprise. From one disaster to another. This promised to be the worst day of my life. Outside Andy was off chasing two crazy poodles. Upstairs Louie was completely out of it. And Jason Teasdale, the last boy my parents would approve of, stood unbudging, with a possessive hand on my shoulder. Let the chips fall where they may, I thought, and prepared for the worst. To my surprise, Mother and Dad emerged from the car laughing.

"Your friend Andy is making a spectacle of himself again," said Mother. She peered at Jason.

"Yeo, babe," he said to her.

My mother's mouth formed a wordless oh. "You one of Louisa's friends?" inquired my dad, looking from me to Jason, to the hand on my shoulder and back again to me.

Jason, who considered adults to be the main source of the overpopulation problem, offered his free hand to Dad. For the second time that day, the gesture was disregarded.

"What are you doing here, young man?" Dad demanded instead. "The girls aren't supposed to have boys over when we're not home." For once I wished Louie would rescue me. "Phew," said Jason, "this town's full of friendly people."

"Jason really has to go," I said, prodding him with my arm. Jason, with his lack of respect for authority, was not likely to sit down and engage in social chit-chat with my father.

"I think I'll go see a man about a dog," said Jason, observing Dad, whose cheeks were puffing like a blow-fish's.

After Jason had climbed on his Harley, revved the motor, and sped off, Mother remarked, "I've seen that fellow around the store. No one from Sand Key drives a motor-cycle like that. He must be a tourist." She emphasized the last word with a frown.

"I'm not sure," I said, practically stumbling over the azalea bush in my eagerness to get inside.

"Not so fast, young lady," Dad said. "What was that boy doing here?"

"He came by to see me," came Louie's voice from the screen door. How long she'd been standing there I don't know. Her quick glance in my direction indicated she wasn't about to give me away. She swayed back and forth a little and grabbed the doorknob for support.

"We don't approve of those rich boys who come down here looking for a good time, Louisa. We don't want him hanging around here getting ideas." Dad pushed his way through the screen as Louie stepped out of his way, the old defiant frown creasing her face.

"Why don't you get off my case," she said. "I don't need your help to choose my friends."

Dad lunged toward her so quickly that I was afraid he

75

might hit her. But he gripped her wrist instead. "Watch your mouth, young lady. I've a good mind to close it for you." They stood glaring at each other, tense as wires about to snap.

"It's not her fault, Dad. Jason is my friend." My words came out muffled, squeaky as a scrambled tape. The four of us stood in the small hallway. Three pairs of eyes focused on me. Feeling the tightness creeping up the back of my neck, I clenched my fists.

Louie came and stood next to me. "Beth has a right to have a boyfriend. Just because she's small doesn't mean she's a baby." I hadn't seen her so fired up for days. But she was defending me this time instead of herself.

"Louisa, you've interfered enough for one day. Keep out of this," Dad ordered. Mother hung back at the door, twisting the handles of her purse. She never disagrees with Dad, but I could tell this time she disapproved.

"Dad, please can we talk about this later when we all calm down?" I pleaded.

"There's nothing more to say," shouted Dad to our retreating backs. "You're not to see that boy again."

"Thanks for trying," I told Louie after I shut the door.

She shrugged. "Forget it." Back to the dull voice, the closed face. I pressed on.

"This family's falling apart. Mom and Dad don't approve of anything we do."

"Correction," said my sister, "they don't approve of anything *I* do. So what else is new?"

The image of Louie floundering around in speech class flashed before my eyes. "You'll have to admit . . ." I started.

Louie interrupted. "They're my parents. They're supposed to love me, no matter what. You too."

"I'm thinking of family pride," I said, "not love."

"Love's more important," Louie said, "so I don't care."

"I wish things were different," I told her.

"Things are different," she replied.

11

———————————

LOUIE IS RIGHT. Love's more important. Unfortunately, my folks don't find her lovable. And Louie doesn't go out of her way to encourage them. I guess she figures why bother. In my case, it's just the opposite. I feel like a jar filled with too much paint. When the top's screwed on, paint seeps over the edges. This is the thing: my folks are trying to keep a lid on me, and I'm absolutely brimming over. I've opted for "love's more important," but it requires sneaking around as if I were a character right out of *The Young and the Restless*. How could I resist Jason? My time with him was so fast-paced I began to think the rest of my life had taken place in slow motion. The minute I climbed behind him on the motorcycle, I had the sense of being swept into a whirlwind.

"What's your father's trip?" asked Jason, when I called him from the storage closet the next day. "Your family's weirder than mine."

"We've been having a few problems lately," I said.

"Why don't you come over, princess? I'll make you forget all about them."

"I'll try," I said, knowing that I'd manage to get to him through a full-scale hurricane. Fortunately, I had no trouble from Dad about going out. He was still bewildered and feeling a little guilty about his reaction to Jason. "It's not that we don't want you to have friends, Beth. We just don't want any surprises."

"I'll be home early." I was eager to see Jason for reasons other than the little ache I felt when we weren't together. Lately, he'd been acting more reckless than usual. It was as if he kept daring himself to go a little further. I was afraid he was getting closer to the edge. He always rode his motorcycle too fast. He barely slept.

I walked and walked through the streets of Sand Key toward Jason's house and thought about him. The air was balmy, sweet-scented with blooming magnolias, and the sky was clear. By now my portfolio was filled with drawings of him. I knew I was storing up memories, that someday he would leave Sand Key, go up North, and this time in our lives would fade into memory.

"Are you going to paint my portrait tonight?" asked Jason, when I reached his house.

"I'm still studying you," I said. Maybe I was being superstitious, but I was afraid to finish his portrait, as if completing it would be the end of us, too.

"Well, study me on the couch," he said, pulling me into the living room. "I feel like snuggling."

"You feel like watching television," I said. His parents had installed a wide-screen set, which made the images practically life-size. *M*A*S*H* had just started, so we settled into the deep cushions to watch. When Klinger appeared dressed in one of his getups, a long dress and a wide-brimmed hat with a plume, Jason broke up. "Maybe I'll use that as a disguise next time I hit the shopping center."

"That's not funny," I said. When the commercial came on, he went to the bar for a beer.

The commercial was odd. No dialogue, just sharp, discordant music in the background. The scene kept shifting from a woman in a trench coat moving through a jewelry store, to a hidden camera, and then to a Monopoly board. Back and forth. The woman fingered merchandise, the camera clicked, and hands moved pieces on the board. The music stopped. The woman slipped a bracelet in her pocket. A voice said, "So you don't think you'll get caught?" Then the camera with the words "You're wrong" flashed on the bottom. Back to the Monopoly game. A card was held up: "Go to Jail." Underneath was the credit. "A paid advertisement by the Retailers Association." Jason stood staring at the screen. He was silent, mashing the can with his fingers and twisting it around.

I wanted to say something, but the words stuck in my throat. I don't believe in omens, but the message was pointing right at us. The card "Go to Jail" almost jumped off the screen, growing in size until its presence dominated the room.

Abruptly Jason switched off the set.

"Getting caught is the bummer," he said, "but they can't do much if you're underage." And the way he said that last remark, slowly with a slight note of disgust, made me realize what I'd suspected all along.

"You didn't get kicked out of school for smoking pot, did you, Jason? You got caught shoplifting." I stood facing him, determined not to let him lie his way out of it.

"O.K., so what if I did. It's hardly a federal case."

"No, just petty larceny," I answered.

"There was a whole group of us. The idea was to see who could walk out with the most stuff. That clip joint in town never missed it. They ripped off students anyway, so why shouldn't we get even?''

"Come off it, Jason. Every time something's missing from our store, it costs my father ten times the amount to make up for it.''

"Tell him to cheat on his expense account or income tax like my father," said Jason glibly.

"You don't know what you're talking about," I said furiously. "You never had to work a day in your life.''

"Oh, come on, Beth, I couldn't help it. I was just overcome with temptation," he said in an exaggerated voice. "I don't know what you're so uptight for. Everybody does it. It's like a game.''

"Well, the game didn't turn out so terrific for you," I countered. "You got expelled from school. How much fun was that?''

"Hell, I laughed in that dip's face when he caught me. And over a lousy pen. Told him to call my lawyer. I knew they wouldn't prosecute me. Not good for public relations. No one in that hick town but preppies can afford their lousy clothes. When he called the school, they had no choice but to suspend me. I'll go back as soon as I feel like it.'' He snapped his fingers. "Just like that. I can't wait to see my father's face when I tell him.''

At this pronouncement, Jason's face grew serious. He shook his head. "What a jerk he is.''

"What about your friends?" I asked. "Did their parents get them out of it, too?''

"Nobody else got caught. The security guard was too busy nabbing me. So they ducked out. My suitemate is back at school hoarding film, wallets, gloves, candy, cigarettes, and every wall soap dispenser in school.'' He punched a pillow with his fist. "He's the richest guy in Connecticut and hasn't paid for a thing in months.'' I could tell the image of his friend safe and sound at school bugged Jason. His mood had turned from cocky assurance to dejection. The evening was ruined. Jason, in a sulk, took me home early, dropping me, as usual, at the corner of Elm, a block from my front door.

12

THURSDAY AFTERNOON, I was supposed to meet Jason after
school. But as I moved through the throngs of kids at the
exit, I didn't see him. No motorcycle. No Jaguar. I searched
the rows of cars with mounting disappointment. Edging
along the lanes of Jeeps and bicycles, I wondered if he'd
forgotten. Maybe he'd fallen asleep on the beach. Maybe he
didn't want to see me again.

As I turned a corner, a large figure blocked my path, a
man wearing a Mexican serape and high sombrero pulled
down over his eyes. He spread his arms out as I cautiously
backed away. I felt as if I'd walked into a tent. He quickly
caught me, and I was enveloped in the coarse material and
the familiar smell of lemon aftershave. "Yeo, babe," came
Jason's voice. As he swung me around, all my senses
quickened. I stood back and regarded him. The hat was
fantastic. Green straw the color of a grass stain, with
embroidered fruit on the band. It rose straight up like a
camel's hump, and the wide brim covered his face. Out of
his mouth protruded a fat cigar.

"How are ya doin', princess?" he said, puffing a smoke ring.

"Great, Jason," I said, freshly awed. "That's quite a hat."

"I've got one for you." From under the vast expanse of his cape he pulled another hat, this one embroidered with flowers. He plunked it on my head, and the hat promptly fell down over my eyes.

"My car's in the shop," he said. "Let's wait for the bus."

"Where are we going?"

"I'm in the mood for an experiment." I knew he didn't mean a science project. He led me over to a bench and began babbling about the new electronic equipment at Neiman-Marcus. "I've always been able to get through chains, locks, mirrors, and tags," said Jason. "But these new surveillance monitors are tricky." The air was heavy with humidity. There were beads of perspiration on Jason's forehead, and his hair curled in damp tendrils around his flushed face.

He ran his sentences together, which made me wonder if he was on something. But I let him keep talking and stared at his hat, trying not to react one way or the other.

"I guess anything you steal is hidden in the hat?" I finally asked, my voice amazingly calm.

He popped the hat up and down quickly a few times. At this point, the sombrero seemed to grow in size like a swollen blister. "Right you are, partner. I'm not going for big items. This is just an experiment to see if I can pull it off. Anyway, I won't keep any of it."

"What if you get caught before you have a chance to return what you've stolen?" I practically screeched.

"Will you keep your voice down," Jason said, gesturing toward a group of kids nearby.

"What happens if you get caught?" I repeated in a low voice, knowing all the while that Jason had no intention of returning anything.

"Oh, they'll drag me into the office and give me some crap about how stealing's a sin. They'll threaten to prosecute and make me a criminal forever. Then they'll try to reach my parents, who are nowhere to be found. Finally, they'll give up and let me go."

"Sounds like you have it all figured out. So why do you want me along? You know I think what you're doing is dumb."

"The only thing that's dumb is not pulling it off. I just want you there to watch out in case anyone notices me. Then all you have to do is twist your hat."

He pulled me to my feet and steered me toward the bus stop. I imagined us sitting on the bus, strands of pearls, scarves, bracelets, and belts dripping out of his hat as if his brains were spilling out. I saw some girls watching us. I could tell they were envious. Jason and I, in our matching sombreros, must have looked like the perfect couple. Yet, for the first time, I wished I could trade places with one of them.

"Don't look at me with that mournful expression," he said. "It spooks me."

"Good. I hope it spooks you into changing your plans."

"Beth, you take things too seriously, as if life is one long list of do's and don't's. Can't you be more spontaneous?"

"I'm trying," I told him, "but lurking around shopping malls hardly brings out the spontaneous side of me." The express bus for Lauderdale came chugging toward us. I tried a new tack.

"Jason, aren't your parents coming here in a few days?"

He nodded. "What about it?"

"After they arrive, you won't have the house to yourself

anymore." The bus rattled to a stop. It was filled with Cubans, workers from the construction site across town. One of the men leaned out the window and shouted, "I like your sombreros, amigos." Jason waved his hat and started to climb aboard. I stood firm on the sidewalk, my arms folded stubbornly to my chest. As the doors swung shut, Jason motioned impatiently. "Come on, Beth." I refused to budge.

"O.K., Romeo and Juliet," said the bus driver. "Make up your minds. I don't have all day." The men on the bus jabbered in Spanish, amused by our version of the balcony scene. The girls across the street stared curiously. Jason kept pushing the doors open; the bus driver kept closing them. Finally Jason, who had shifted his irritation to the bus driver, muttered a curse and jumped off. The Cubans applauded and cheered. *"Viva el amor. Viva el amor."* Jason, loving the attention, popped the sombrero down over my eyes and pretended to tackle me. I fell hard against him, and for a moment, encased in his arms, I was almost happy again. But just as suddenly as he grabbed me, he let go and went striding off in the opposite direction. I ran to catch up, which made the group of girls snicker and the Cubans shout with laughter as the bus pulled away. Yet I knew I had won. Jason's shopping spree would have to wait for another day.

We took the next bus to his house. He scrunched himself into a seat opposite me and refused to talk. I tried desperately to think of a way to salvage the afternoon. We had ended last night on a sour note. I didn't want to make things worse, but I knew we were building to a major battle. Any attempts at conversation failed. Jason wouldn't respond.

I couldn't believe it when we walked into his house. The living room was a shambles. "What happened after you took me home last night?" There were beer cans and dirty dishes strewn everywhere. The ashtrays overflowed with cigarette butts. The place had a smoky, rancid smell.

"Had a few friends over," he mumbled, contrite all of a sudden. "Some guys I met at a bar."

"What if your parents walked in and found this mess?" I sounded like an indignant wife. "You don't care, do you?" I suspected he wanted them to find the house a disaster area just to get a rise out of them. I stomped around, collecting ashtrays, tossing cans in the wastebasket. "Where's the broom?" I demanded. That's when he started to laugh.

"You look hilarious, banging about ferociously like Minnie Mouse. Don't get so angry, Beth. Here, I'll help you." He produced a mop and began swinging it in the air enthusiastically.

"I think you're a complete psycho," I said. He trotted behind me, making haphazard attempts to help. Against my better judgment, I began to soften. "I think you ought to see a shrink," I said finally in exasperation when he collapsed on the rug in mock exhaustion.

"The house isn't that bad." He laughed. "I don't need a shrink just because I hate to clean up."

"Jason Teasdale, you know exactly what I'm getting at."

Scowling, he grabbed me roughly around the legs and tried to pull me down. "I can think of better things to do than talk about doctors or pick up trash."

"Cut it out, Jason. I mean it." I managed to keep my balance.

"If anyone needs a shrink, it's someone a lot closer to you than me. Why don't you go home and pick on that crazy sister of yours?"

"What are you getting at? Tell me!" I demanded.

"Your sister's a hopeless case. She even showed up here one night."

My stomach started to churn. "What did she want?"

"She started accusing me of all kinds of stupid things. Believe me, I set her straight. I'm beginning to think you're just as crazy!"

"You don't care about anyone, do you, Jason?"

"Look, don't lay the blame on me. It's not my fault you and your sister are screwed up." Opponents on opposite sides of a net, we threw words back and forth, our voices rising and falling like tennis balls. I could tell by the brittle edge to his voice that he was about to come in for the kill, to score set point.

"I've had it with your little-girl ideas. Grow up! It's a big bad world out there. Maybe Louie likes to be wild. Maybe I like to shoplift. You're really a bore with that innocent Miss Goody-Goody stuff."

"Don't do this," I begged. "You don't mean that."

"Bye, bye, Miss American Pie," he snarled. "You're just too sweet for me, lady."

"I swear I'll walk out and never come back," I said. I waited a few seconds, hoping he would try to stop me. But as I turned to go, he looked away with a sneer and pushed the button to open the bar.

I stumbled out. It was a relief to climb on the bus, take the back seat, and cry alone all the way back to town.

13

BY THE TIME the bus let me off on Main Street, I'd recovered enough to stop sobbing, but I definitely had a bad case of the hiccups. My reflection in the window as the bus pulled off revealed a red and swollen face. What a mess! Head lowered, I hurried home, praying I wouldn't run into anyone I knew. But as luck would have it, I spotted Andy sitting on the curb in front of Mr. Feely's pharmacy. He was slurping a chocolate ice-cream cone.

"What's up?" he asked, as I tried to sneak by him. "You look as if you've lost your best friend, which by the way you've been acting lately doesn't mean me." I'd been avoiding him since the last dog episode.

I hiccupped loudly and felt a tear drip down my cheek. I kept on walking. Andy fell in step beside me and patted me on the back.

"Want to hear my latest tale, spelled t-a-i-l?" he asked.

"Let's hear it. You'll tell me, anyway."

"You wouldn't have believed the mutts yesterday. My mother has a spaz every time she sees them. 'Come here, you itsy-bitsy poopsie-woopsies,' she says in this dumb baby voice. They took one look at her, lifted up their little legs, and lathered her in unison. A real waterfall! Boy, was she a mess."

"Spare me the gory details," I pleaded, hiccupping and laughing at the same time. Only Andy could cheer me up at a time like this.

"She just stood there dripping. I handed her the leashes and said, 'The poopsie-woopsies are all yours.' I think my days as a dog walker may be numbered."

"I hope so. I don't think I can take another dog t-a-i-l."

"Beth, may I ask you something?"

I hiccupped out an incoherent "sure." Andy wrinkled his nose and brushed the flap of hair off his forehead. He shifted from one foot to another.

"Do you think I'm attractive? I mean to, um, to other people, like girls?" He couldn't look me in the eye. I almost laughed again, but I knew he was serious.

"Well, if you cleaned up your act a little. Maybe buy a new shirt other than one that says *Florida is the Sunshine State*." I looked him up and down. "And other than your slacks, you'll do in a pinch. Why?"

"There's this girl I met the other day. I spotted her at the drugstore. She's even shorter than I am. I'm trying to work up the nerve to ask her out." I felt depressed all over again. And the hiccups stopped. Andy's news scared them right out of me. Even he was about to have a girlfriend. What if he started spending all his time with her? I'd be more alone than ever. No Jason and no Andy. But I tried to look encouraging.

"Maybe you should call her. What's the worst that could happen?"

"She could say no. Then I'll go bury my head in the sand."

"Do you really like her?" I asked in a small voice. He gave me a funny look.

"You know I like short girls," he said. "Hey, cheer up, Beth." He grabbed my hand and squeezed it. His was sticky from the ice cream, but no one's hand had ever felt so good to me. Sniffling, I held on as if our fingers were glued together. Then my throat tightened, and the hiccups started all over again. Andy pried his hand loose and pounded me hard on the back.

"Watch it!" I cried. "I'm not a punching bag."

"You're in bad shape, that's for sure. Are you going to tell me what's wrong?"

Shaking my head, I said, "It's time for me to make my ungraceful exit."

"Disgraceful is more like it," said Andy, giving me one last thump.

At home, Louie was sunning herself on the porch. To prevent her skin from burning, she'd glopped at least a tube of Coppertone on herself. Tonight she would rub in so much moisturizer it would be like sleeping in the same room with a seal. But at least she was speaking to me again.

"Is today your day off?" I asked, hoping she had quit instead.

"Yes," came her sleepy reply. I wanted to beg her to come back to the store, which I'm quickly turning into a worse disaster area than Jason's house. But she's too stubborn to listen.

"Jason and I are through," I blurted.

She sat up with a start. "You're kidding!" She sounded

so happy I didn't elaborate. I just lay down on the grass and blubbered some more until Louie snorted, "Don't be such a nerd. He's not worth it."

If he's not worth it, I felt like asking, what were you doing over at his house? Instead, I gave one last sniffle and went inside.

14

AT SCHOOL the next morning, I wandered about in a complete daze, as if the familiar halls had turned into strange corridors leading nowhere. In the time it took to walk down two flights of stairs to the art studio, three people asked me how Jason was. The first time I said, "Just great," in a cheery voice; the second, I shrugged. The third time, when Louie's friend Susie Sloan inquired, "What's new with the incredible hunk?" I was practically in tears. Being notorious had totally lost its appeal.

In art class, I couldn't concentrate. Pushing the clay around like a glob of Silly Putty, I was conscious only of a terrible ache, as if I'd lost an arm or a leg. Thoughts about Jason filled my head, pounded away at me. How could I get him out of my mind? Maybe I needed an exorcist? Destroy the evidence. That phrase kept repeating itself. Get rid of all traces of Jason. That might erase him from my memory. Then I remembered the drawings. Burgundy Blues still had my sketchbook. What if she'd already submitted it?—Jason practically naked on the beach for my parents and the whole world to see.

I diddled around for the rest of the period until finally I had the nerve to approach her. "Miss Blues, can I talk to you for a second?" She was setting an odd assortment of clay shoes, our latest project, into the kiln. Wiping dust off her hands, she held up a clay sandal. "Isn't this marvelous? One of my ninth-graders made it. I really believe we're all born imaginative. It's society that inhibits our creativity."

Don't go off on an aesthetic tangent, I silently told her. Once she started, she'd babble on, the bell would ring, and I'd lose my nerve.

Quickly I blurted, "I want my portfolio back." With one hand on her hip, Miss Blues regarded me with raised eyebrows. "I'm not ready to show my work."

"I haven't sent it in yet," she said. "To be honest, I fully expected you to turn in more drawings."

"I don't have any more."

"Did I discourage you by my critique? I didn't mean to. You show more promise than any student I've ever had."

"No, that's not it. I just don't want anyone to see those particular pictures." Emily Dickinson's poem "I'm nobody" went through my mind.

> *How dreary—to be—somebody!*
> *How public—like a frog—*
> *To tell one's name—the livelong June—*
> *To an admiring bog!*

"Miss Blues," I pleaded, "I don't need to be public like a frog!"

"Yes, Beth. I know that poem. But you don't need to hide, to isolate yourself like Emily Dickinson. Think of the pleasure we get from reading her poems. I like to imagine her life would have been happier had she known how admired she was to become."

"I don't want the attention," I insisted. "I don't need to be famous. Besides, my parents will never let me go to summer school, especially when they see the pictures. I don't need to go to school. I can draw anywhere—on the beach, in my special room. People don't have to see what I do. And the pictures of Jason, they just . . . upset me."

"Is it the boy who posed for the pictures?" she asked gently. "Is that what's worrying you?" I nodded and burst into tears. I cried as if my heart were breaking. I felt that I was being torn into pieces.

There were too many people pulling me—my parents in one direction, Jason in another, and even Miss Blues was pressuring me. In the midst of it all I felt small, as insignificant as one of my tiny pieces of colored glass.

"Beth, I'm not going to make you do anything you don't want to do. And if you can't talk about that boy now, if you must keep that private, I understand. Everyone has a right to their secrets. But I'll ask you one question: What do you really want? Before you cancel out, think hard! You're not a pawn on a chessboard to be moved forward or backward at someone else's whim. Beth Goodall, you are your own person."

"I don't want to hurt my parents," I said lamely. "And I want Jason Teasdale out of my head."

"All right. I know you feel boxed in." From under the debris of papers, folders, books, and files, she pulled out the portfolio and handed it back to me. "Sometimes," she said, "I wonder what I'm doing in this business. Maybe I'll give up teaching and become a plumber."

Along the corridor hung the science class's collection of flowers and butterflies trapped behind glass. Rows of dead brown roses and flattened wings. "You feel boxed in," Miss Blues had said. Was I as boxed in as those butterflies displayed on the wall? No way, I thought. I'm not going to let that happen to me. The days when a timid girl hid in the closet drawing her fantasies, daydreaming her life away, were long gone, and I wasn't willing to go back. But I didn't know how to move forward.

That night I took one last look at my drawings, fully intending to burn them. But when I held a lighted match to the paper, I ended up blowing it out. Twenty minutes after I pitched the portfolio in the trashcan, I retrieved it. Finally I shoved the notebook into the drawer in the storage closet. Destroying the evidence wasn't going to work.

15

THE WEEKEND came and passed. No call from Jason. At first, I was so angry I didn't care. I told myself he was just a spoiled rich kid, a rotten jerk. But every time the phone rang I jumped. I wandered around town looking for his motorcycle, hoping to catch a glimpse of him. I must have called his house a dozen times. But as soon as I heard his Northern drawl, I hung up. I heard rumors, though. Louie accidentally-on-purpose mentioned he'd been going to some beach parties. I thought I saw him one day with a girl in his car. I had dreams about him. In one dream, I rang his doorbell. He answered all out of breath. He wasn't wearing a shirt. A girl was lying on the couch, laughing. It was Louie. He closed the door in my face. I woke up with tears in my eyes.

When no one was home, I'd dig out the St. Christopher's medal, twisting the gold chain around my finger. I imagined a hundred conversations with Jason. He would call and apologize or turn up at school. He'd tell me he was going to fall apart if I didn't forgive him. But nothing happened.

Finally on Friday night after a miserable week, Louie

said, "You're making weird moaning noises in your sleep. Keeps me awake half the night. Call Jason. And this time don't hang up!"

For Louie, I told myself as I picked up the phone and dialed Jason's number. My hand was shaking. A strange voice answered. A female. My words stuck in my throat.

"Hello," she said, stringing out the "o" in a modulated accent.

"May I speak to Jason?" I said, so softly that she had to say hello again, this time very impatiently.

"It's for you, Jason," she finally said, in such a huffy tone that I knew it must be his mother.

"It's Beth," I managed to whisper. "I'd like to talk to you."

"Oh, yeah?"

"How about tomorrow?" I said after an awkward silence.

"I'll meet you in the square around noon," Jason agreed, but he didn't sound thrilled. I hadn't expected wild enthusiasm, but Jason's voice seemed a million miles away. Falling asleep that night was almost impossible. Instead of moaning in my sleep, I remained wide-awake and groaned out loud. Louie had to throw her pillow to quiet me down.

"I'm seeing Jason tomorrow," I whispered.

Louie held the pillow over my head. "Maybe I should put you out of your misery now."

Saturday morning. Mother handed Louie and me a list of chores. "I'm not sure I have time," said Louie. "They put me on a double shift at work." Unfortunately, my date with Jason wasn't a better excuse.

"I'm not a policewoman, Louisa. If you can't get these simple tasks done, forget it." Louie looked like a puppy who had just been spanked for no reason.

"She's really been working a lot lately," I said.

"Then you handle it, Beth," said Mother, giving me both lists.

"But I made plans. I can't . . ."

"I don't know what to make of you, Beth," Dad said.

Louie took the lists back from me. "Forget it. If you give me the car, I'll take care of it." They argued back and forth until Dad finally said, "Come on, then, Louisa. Drop us off at the store." I gave my sister a grateful look.

As soon as the car pulled off, I dashed to the closet and began flinging clothes around. My wardrobe consists of T-shirts, paint-splattered jeans, and boring cotton skirts. I went through Louie's side and finally settled on a white sundress and her three-inch sandals.

Twelve o'clock finally came. I tottered down the block on my sister's sandals. Jason was waiting in the Jaguar. His hair had bleached almost white in the sun, his tan was deeper than ever.

"Yeo, babe." He smiled, but his eyes were cold. I felt scared. He didn't even get out to open the door for me.

I stumbled over my heels and practically fell into the front seat. So much for sexy! I was off to a clumsy start. Jason drove very fast without speaking. He smoked a cigarette, taking short, quick puffs.

It took all the courage I could muster to say finally, "I've missed you." No response. "I guess you've been busy with your parents here," I continued. He scowled and flicked his cigarette. I watched the wind carry it away.

"They haven't even bothered to call the school yet. Mother's too busy planning her social life, Dad's on the phone with his broker, and little Jason is out loose on the streets of Sand Key."

I didn't like the way he said that. "What do you mean?"

"This town gets so boring, I can't take it. I'm dying to go back North." Only a few weeks ago, he wanted to stay. Because of me.

"What have you been doing?"

"The usual. I have some Christmas shopping to do. Want to come along?" Jason's idea of Christmas spirit is taking, not giving. But if I said no, he'd drop me off and I'd never see him again.

"Let's stay away from that fancy shopping center," I said. "I've had nightmares about that place."

"Bag it, will you? If you can't cope, forget it!" He'd lapsed into his prep-school lingo. There was no way to reason with him. He raced the motor and sped down the highway until we reached the million-dollar parking lot.

"Why do we have to do this?" I asked.

"Look, princess. Do you want to stick with me or not?"

"I want to be with you," I said, "but not here."

Jason fidgeted, eyeing the windows gleaming with gold ornaments, watches and rings, sequined gowns, and crystal goblets. A mannequin in a bikini was perched on a silver sleigh. "Frosty the Snowman" blared from a loudspeaker, filling the parking lot with Christmas cheer. Fake snow in the windows. Fake cheer in the hot, sandy streets.

"No one's twisting your arm to stay," said Jason. But how could I back out now? I'd waited so long to see him again. Maybe I could conjure up a diversion.

"I'm staying," I said, but my voice was as shaky as my spiked heels.

Jason opened his trunk and pulled out the huge sombrero. He grabbed me around the waist and danced in a circle. "Cheer up, princess. We'll celebrate on the beach later." Jason's gay mood wasn't contagious. My stomach felt queasy.

He handed me a carpetbag. I handed it back.

"They've installed all kinds of contraptions in Z's," he said. "Mirrors on the ceiling, plastic tabs on the clothes, and buzzers."

"You're hardly inconspicuous in that garb," I said. He shrugged, that funny look on his face again. I wanted to grab Jason, shake him out of this craziness.

Z's was jammed with people and merchandise. Shoppers thronged up and down the aisles. Jason examined a cashmere sweater. He quickly scanned the area. Although we were surrounded by people, no one paid any attention to us. His hands shook as he shoved the sweater into his carpetbag.

"My father will love finding this under the tree," he said. Then he tipped his hat and scratched his ear. In went a gold lighter and cufflinks.

I saw a man in a dark suit watching us. "Over there, Jason," I said. "That man!"

"Cool it! He's not going to stop us." Jason handed me a pair of jeans. "Why don't you try these on, princess?" he said loudly. The way he said my nickname made me cringe. The man was walking toward Jason. Quickly I grabbed the carpetbag and rushed back to the fitting room. Down the long corridor, past the dressing rooms, I found myself in a storage area.

A saleswoman stood wrapping packages. She looked me up and down. Feeling dizzy with fear, I clutched the carpetbag. I felt as if it were permanently cemented to my fingers.

"Where did you come from?" she asked, glancing at the sack.

"I was just trying on a pair of Levi's. They were too big. My friend's meeting me outside."

"What's in that?" She pointed suspiciously.

"Just some stuff," I answered, praying she wouldn't

pursue the subject, inching my way toward the door. A gust of cold air from the vent made me shiver. Outside, the sun blazed as teenagers in sports cars gunned their motors and drag-raced around the parking lot. A group of little boys licking snowcones ran past the window. Freedom was only two steps away.

"Perhaps you'd better let me take a look. Just for security purposes," she said brusquely. I started to argue, but her grim, disapproving frown stopped me in mid-sentence. My ears buzzed with a terrible pressure, and my hands trembled.

As I heaved the bag onto the wooden counter, the lady pushed a button. Almost immediately a man in a gray uniform emerged from the basement. A silver badge gleamed on his chest. "What have we got here?" he asked.

By now, I'd become a silent witness to my own downfall. My mind was blank as paper, my body a mass of prickly sensations. The saleswoman retrieved the sweater, with its red tag dribbling out of the pocket like drops of blood. She let out a triumphant snort.

"Did you steal this?" asked the man, whose name tag read Walter Sly, an appropriate name, I thought, for a thief nabber. I shrugged my shoulders. "No sales slip," he said. I looked down. "Young lady, you were just caught red-handed. If I were you, I'd confess before you get yourself in worse trouble."

"I didn't steal anything," I insisted.

"Well, who did?" the lady asked, her face bobbing indignantly toward me, her finger wagging in my face. "How did these things happen to get in your bag?"

I avoided her eyes, all the time wondering where Jason was. I didn't expect him to rescue me—not really—but I kept hoping he'd suddenly appear, crying, "This girl's innocent. Lock me up instead."

"I suggest you come downstairs." Mr. Sly guided me firmly by the arm. The trudge down felt like a descent into hell. The security office was a small brown cubicle—bare except for a metal desk, a chair, and file cabinets. Gloves, handbags, blouses, and underwear were piled in a corner. "Sit there." I sank down and closed my eyes. Mr. Sly picked up the phone. "I'm about to call the police. If you aren't willing to make a statement, I'll press charges."

He'd never believe the real story, and I couldn't turn Jason in. "O.K.," I said. "I did it."

"Did what?" He wasn't going to make it easy for me.

"I took the sweater and the jeans."

"Were you with anyone else? Our floorman reported a boy behaving suspiciously, too." Startled, I looked up. Did he know? Had he nabbed Jason? I shook my head.

"No, no, I was by myself."

"What's your name? Do you have any identification? How old are you? Is this the first time you've been caught?" He was thumbing through a file, and the questions kept flying like guided missiles.

I answered in dull tones. "Beth Goodall, 1044 Palm Street. I'm fifteen."

"You look young for your age."

"Yes, I know." I paused. "This is the first time."

He sat on the edge of the desk, observing me with an almost sympathetic look. "Why did you do this?"

"I don't know." My voice sounded flat, expressionless. Why? I asked myself. Because a beautiful boy named Jason called me princess? What kind of a stupid, infantile reason was that? I didn't know why. All I knew was that I'd diverted myself right into trouble. My diversion days were over.

"Look, Beth, I'm going to give you a break. It's your first offense. If we prosecuted every shoplifter we caught, we'd be buried in paperwork, and the jails would be overflowing. If your parents will come for you and will accept responsibility, I'll let you go with a warning."

A new fear like an electric shock went through me at the thought of calling my parents. He handed me the phone. I stared into the receiver and dialed slowly. The phone rang four times before Louie answered in a bored voice. "Let me talk to Dad," I said quickly.

"They're not here. They went shopping." She hung up.

Mr. Sly narrowed his eyes when I had to call back. "Louie, how soon will they be home?"

"I don't know. What's the problem?"

"Hold on. Don't hang up." I turned to Mr. Sly. "I have an older sister. Can she come for me?"

"Tell her to get over here right away."

"Where are you?" Louie was saying. I could picture her, probably curled up in bed, doing her nails, irritated by my interruption. "I'm about to leave," she said. "Take a bus."

"Louie, I can't explain now, but I'm in big trouble. Just come over here. I'm at Z's, down in the security office." I was choking on the words.

"What?" she said. "Is this a joke?"

"Please, Louie." I was pleading now.

"All right, all right, I'll be right there." Thank God she was going to come through for me.

I slumped in the chair and avoided looking at Mr. Sly, who, I could tell, was scrutinizing me. Every minute seemed like an hour. I imagined being dragged from Z's with a crowd of people jeering. Finally, Louie was standing at the door, an amazed look on her face. She was all dressed up and looked about thirty.

"Did you steal these things?" Mr. Sly repeated in front of Louie.

"Yes."

"All right; go on, then. If we catch you here again, we'll let the police take over."

A moment later I was outside. The sun's harsh glare made me blink. Then I realized my eyes were filled with tears. Louie drove carefully, not saying much. She let me babble on until I managed to spill the whole story.

"Dammit, I hope they lock that Jason Teasdale up and throw away the key. I never should have listened to him," she said hoarsely.

"Listened to him? What do you mean?"

"How do you think I met Jason in the first place?" she asked. "He came into the hardware store a couple of times. He looked around but never bought anything. We flirted alot. I figured he was coming in to see me. But I started watching him. One day I caught him ripping off a chain saw. Can you imagine? A big item like that! He must have thought I was an idiot not to notice."

"What did you do?"

"I didn't do anything at first. But when he started to leave, I said, 'Do you want to pay by check or cash?' Well, he didn't even flinch. He wrote out a check and left. Later, he was waiting for me in the Jag. Took me to his house and put on a big snow job. I guess I had a little crush on him. He swore he'd never steal from the store again, but I didn't believe him. We had fights about it until . . ." Her voice trailed off. Until me, she meant.

"When you started dating him," she continued, "I didn't know what to do. I should have told you about him right away."

"It wouldn't have made any difference, Louie."

"That's what I figured. When I went over to Jason's and warned him to leave you alone, he just laughed."

"What did he say?" There was a hard knot in my throat.

Louie paused. "He said, 'Go ahead and tell her. I don't care.'"

We didn't talk much after that. When the car came to a sudden jolting stop, I knew we were home. "I have to go to work," Louie said in a dull tone that let me know she dreaded it.

I leaned over and hugged her tight, holding on as the tears fell. When I looked at my sister, she was crying, too. "I love you, Louie."

"Me too," she said. "Now go inside and calm down."

Alone in the house, I took refuge in the storage closet. Over and over I studied my sketches of Jason. I spread them out on the floor. There were at least thirty drawings, quick studies on 10 x 12 white paper. I lined them up side by side, examining the expressions and positions of the figures until the image of Jason, the person, got lost, replaced by lines and shapes, the movement of one drawing next to another. For the first time in a while, I had an urge to draw. I grabbed a roll of brown wrapping paper from the corner, tore off a large sheet, and started working. It was as if I'd been listening to Muzak blaring in an elevator, and now a completely different sound came blasting forth. If only I could transfer my feelings onto paper. Maybe I could reveal something new. The charcoal began dancing to the music in my head, dancing across the page. What emerged was a portrait of Jason, abstracted from all the other images of him—a mass of darks and lights, curves and angles. Bent over on the floor, I rubbed the thick lines with my fist, extending the thin lines. I worked and worked until my hand stopped moving and the sounds in my head subsided. No longer a picture-postcard-perfect boy, Jason was revealed as a real flesh-and-blood person, angry and defiant, distant but lost at the same time.

Nearly five o'clock, judging by the fading light through

the window. Quickly I stuffed the drawings, including the new one, into a cardboard portfolio and tied them with a string. I remembered Miss Blues's question "What do you want?" What I wanted, I realized, was to do my work. If my parents, Jason, or even Louie and Andy were disappointed with me, I would feel sad, even terrible, but I could survive. Yet, if I couldn't draw, if someone took away my charcoals and paints, it would be like taking away my breathing space. Then I really would be Nobody.

One more step to take, and that was dropping the folder on Burgundy Blues's desk at school. The decision to do that had a calming effect on me. The project was over, at least my part of it. And my brooding about Jason Teasdale III? That was over, too.

16

WHEN LOUIE delivered the fat envelope, I was hiding in the basement of the store behind a roll of chicken wire. First came the thump of her footsteps and then the familiar husky voice. "Squirt, what are you doing?"

I peered over my barricade. "How'd you know where I was?"

"Mom told me. It seems you spend a lot of time in this hole," she said, regarding my makeshift drawing board of two-by-fours. I didn't realize they'd noticed I was missing. Guilty as I felt for avoiding my duties, upstairs I was useless, either sneezing or bungling some minor chore.

"This place is going downhill," Louie said. "I've never seen it so disorganized."

"It's not my fault," I grumbled. The truth was that Louie used to take care of details that Mom and Dad couldn't get to. Without her, things didn't run as smoothly. Even the customers were complaining. Everyone seemed to miss Louie except my parents. How could they be so totally dense?

Louie waved the letter. "This came in the mail. Looks very interesting."

I could see the return address. Florida State University. Whether the letter contained good news or bad, I was still afraid to open it. A rejection from art school would be terrible. But even worse would be a scholarship I might not be able to accept.

"Well, if you're going to stand there like a dummy, I'll open it," said my sister, proceeding to tear the seal.

"Give it to me," I cried. My fingers started to tingle. There it was in black and white: "Congratulations, we are pleased to offer you a place in our summer program." The letter went on to say that tuition and art supplies would be included. My chest felt so tight I had to take a deep breath. I guess I started shaking, because Louie put her hand on my arm and said, "Take it easy. Let me look." Quickly she scanned the letter. "Beth, this is terrific. I'm really excited for you." I gulped back a sob. "What's the matter?"

I pointed upstairs, where my real world, the world of my parents, spread before me in rows of nails, nuts, and bolts. "Ohhh," Louie said slowly, realization creeping into her voice. "Well, what are you going to do? Do you want to go?"

I sank down on the burlap bags of grass seed. "Yes, more than anything else in the world."

"Then you'd better go up there and tell them." She motioned me toward the stairs.

"I can't. I just can't do it."

"Why not? What's so terrible about saying what you want?"

"I'm afraid they'll think I'm deserting them."

"You mean you're afraid they'll say no," said Louie in a contemptuous tone. "And if you do something they don't like, you won't be their sweet little Beth anymore."

109

"That's not fair. I get along with them because I try."

"You don't think I've tried?" said Louie. "They have a preference, and it's not for me."

"Louie, if you came back to work here, maybe they'd let me go to summer school."

"It's too late for that," said Louie.

"Why? Why is it too late? You hate working at Ace. You always come home in such a bad mood."

"Look, I don't know the customers there. And the manager sticks me with a lot of busy work. But at least I'm appreciated." I couldn't argue with that.

"What's going on down there?" came my father's booming voice. "Beth, come upstairs and give us a hand." Clutching the letter, I went upstairs to help my parents. The store was filled with customers. Mom and Dad's pre-Christmas sale brought out practically every bargain-hunting do-it-yourselfer in town. People milled about, fingering the disorganized heaps of merchandise and looking confused. Mrs. Johnson, who specializes in painted birdhouses that double as purses for the tourists, grumbled and complained. The minute she spotted Louie, she grabbed her. "There you are, young lady. I need parts, and you're the only one who can find them," she brayed.

"Not me," said Louie, fixing Mrs. Johnson with a disinterested stare. "I don't work here anymore."

"Don't give me that nonsense. I need small paintbrushes and four-inch wood slats, and you'd better get cracking."

Louie turned to my parents, who were tearing around, trying in vain to keep up with the crowds. Dad shot her a pleading glance. That was all it took to send Louie into immediate action. Pretty soon the whole family, including me, was engaged in the business of the day, and I realized my personal business would have to wait.

Three hours later, after the last customer departed and the cash register clanged shut for the final time, we collapsed together, exhausted. Louie sprawled on the counter, I slumped on the floor, and my parents sank down on two empty crates. My father grabbed my mother's hand. "We did it," he cried. "The sale has brought us out of our slump. Thanks," he said, "you did a great job." Neither of my parents was looking directly at Louie, but I knew Dad's remark was meant for her.

"Mom and Dad, after the total waste case I've made of myself at the store, I think you need Louie back."

Louie's face was a study, her eyes sad, her mouth twisted with anger. "They don't think so."

"Why don't you tell Louie how you really feel? She's the one who deserves the credit today."

Dad walked over to Louie and put his arm around her. "Welcome back," he said.

Louie shook her head. "Look, I have to work to-night."

"Mother and I have been meaning to talk to you about that," Dad said. "We need you here with us."

"Thanks, Dad, but I can't do that. Not now."

"Why not?" Dad asked, his voice gruff.

Louie gripped the counter as if she thought it might collapse any minute. "The manager at Ace's wants to put me in their training program when I graduate. It will give me enough money to get out on my own."

"Are you going to take it?" I practically shrieked, my heart sinking into my stomach. My parents, who usually react to Louie instead of understanding her, said nothing.

No screaming or accusations, just downcast looks and silence.

"Is that what you want to do?" Dad finally asked.

"No," Louie said softly. "Not really."

"This store's called Goodall Hardware," Dad said. "You're a Goodall. You belong here, Louisa. We'll try to work things out." My sister nodded.

"Then it's settled," said Mother. "Now we're one big happy family."

One big happy family except for one person, I thought. If I didn't speak up now, I never would. I handed Dad the letter. "I have somewhere I want to go, too," I said.

"We can't afford to lose you now, Beth," said Dad, handing the letter back without reading it.

"Don't do that to me," I cried.

Mother stepped forward. "O.K., Beth, what is it you want to do?"

"It's not a question of what she wants to do," Dad interjected.

"I think it is," I said. "And it's a question of what I have to do. I want to be an artist. I have a chance to find out if I'm good enough."

"You are good enough," said Louie. "And now that I'll be working again . . ." She stood on the sidelines as if she were a cheerleader rooting for me to go the final distance. But I knew she couldn't rescue me, nor I her. Not anymore. No one could make things happen for me except myself. So I put the letter back in Dad's hands, and this time he read it. I could hear my watch ticking.

Finally, after he and Mother handed the letter back and forth, he said, "I guess we can spare you. You spend more time in the basement, anyway." Then we were all talking at once. I filled in the details, laughing, crying, and jumping around.

"Beth, someday, when you're a great artist," Louie said, "be sure you buy your art supplies from Goodall Hardware."

"We don't sell art supplies," Dad said.

"We will now," said my sister.

Postscript

THE LAST TIME I saw Jason was on the front page of the *Sand Key Chronicle*. There are other images of him that stay in my mind as permanent and frozen in time as that photograph: Jason on his Harley, Jason at the market, on the beach, or behind the wheel of his Jag. Jason wearing his sombrero, Jason shoving the carpetbag at me. For a while, I imagined him wandering around Z's forever in that big hat. But the only real photograph I have of him was taken the day he left Sand Key.

Christmas Eve, Officer Muncie caught him carrying a case of wine out of a liquor store in broad daylight. How could Jason have believed he wouldn't get caught? A minor, strutting down Main Street with twelve bottles of rosé? I guess he knew he wouldn't get away with it; he didn't really want to.

According to the *Chronicle*, they searched his house and found piles of stolen goods in his basement. He'd never eaten the candy, returned the jewelry, or worn anything in the cartons stuffed with clothes. The police returned several tools to my parents' store.

After that the story gets fuzzy. Maybe Mr. Teasdale bribed the judge or used his influence; maybe they promised to take him North for psychiatric care. But the Teasdales left town. Their house on Outer Beach Road sits vacant with a FOR SALE sign in front. In the newspaper clipping, Jason is glaring defiantly at the photographer, while Officer Muncie gloats officiously. His parents, handsome and well dressed, have their backs to the camera. Now they have to pay attention to Jason. There's no choice.

My parents, who insisted on framing my prize-winning drawings, might have recognized his picture, but they didn't say anything. They were in a good mood because of the Christmas season. The store is doing well, and now that Louie is back, Mom and Dad aren't so overworked. I pitch in when I can, but I still have sneezing fits. Sometimes my parents fall back in their old pattern of picking on Louie and treating me like a baby. But they discuss business with Louie for hours and even follow some of her suggestions. Shopping has always been her specialty.

On New Year's Day, Louie asked, "Beth, have you made your New Year's resolutions?"

"I never keep my resolutions. So what's the point?"

"I've got a super idea. Why don't we sit down and write lists. Stuff them in two bottles to toss into the sea." Louie is a closet romantic.

"What a terrific idea!" I said. "Once Andy put a note in a Coke bottle and threw it into the bay. Six months later, he received a letter from a man in Australia who found it washed up on shore."

Louie produced two bottles, one an empty Hawaiian Punch and the other Jack Daniels. "I know which one's yours." I laughed, and began composing my list. First, I put the usual things like "Be more helpful around the house"; "Don't be rude to Mother when she nags"; "Work harder at math instead of doodling"; and so on. It sounded like the Ten Commandments. But my last vow for the new year was "Next time I fall in love, pick someone more like Andy."

Louie was peering over my shoulder. "Someone more like Andy," she read. "How about Andy himself?"

"A definite maybe," I admitted, folding the paper and stuffing it in the bottle. But as we started off, a thought occurred to me. "Hold on, Louie, I forgot something." I ran up to my room and dug through my wicker basket. Then we were off on the familiar trail, cutting through driveways and back yards until we came to Main Street, then across the highway toward the ocean.

The beach was jammed with sunbathers. They sat in clumps, rubbing each other with oil. Little kids chased seagulls and dug castles in the sand. Clouds seemed to pass over the sun at the right moment, just when the rays were too intense. Tourists get their money's worth out of a day like today.

Louie and I made our way over shovels, pails, towels, and bodies to a private spot in front of a craggy rock.

"You first," I told her.

"Together," she said. Side by side, we tossed the bottles into the Gulf. They bobbed for a moment, as if they were anchored, until a huge wave carried them off.

I had placed the St. Christopher's medal in the bottle. Like Jason, it was out of my life forever, traveling to places unknown. The patron saint of wanderers. Let it protect itself. As for me, no longer "a cricket on the hearth content to stay at home," I'm traveling forward, too, but under my own protection, at my own speed.

About the Author

BYE, BYE, MISS AMERICAN PIE is Jan Greenberg's fifth book for young readers. She lives and works in St. Louis, Missouri where she is involved in Arts Education at Webster University, specifically theater, visual arts and poetry. Ms. Greenberg has three teenage daughters who have inspired her work.